For

MORTAL CHAOS
DEEP
OBLIVION

All best wishes,

Also by Matt Dickinson

Mortal Chaos

MATT DICKINSON

MORTAL CHAOS
DEEP OBLIVION

OXFORD

UNIVERSITY PRESS

OXFORD
UNIVERSITY PRESS

Great Clarendon Street, Oxford OX2 6DP

Oxford University Press is a department of the University of Oxford.
It furthers the University's objective of excellence in research, scholarship,
and education by publishing worldwide in

Oxford   New York

Auckland   Cape Town   Dar es Salaam   Hong Kong   Karachi
Kuala Lumpur   Madrid   Melbourne   Mexico City   Nairobi
New Delhi   Shanghai   Taipei   Toronto

With offices in

Argentina   Austria   Brazil   Chile   Czech Republic   France   Greece
Guatemala   Hungary   Italy   Japan   Poland   Portugal   Singapore
South Korea   Switzerland   Thailand   Turkey   Ukraine   Vietnam

Oxford is a registered trade mark of Oxford University Press
in the UK and in certain other countries

British Library Cataloguing in Publication Data

Data available

ISBN: 978-0-19-275715-9

1 3 5 7 9 10 8 6 4 2

Printed in Great Britain
Paper used in the production of this book is a natural,
recyclable product made from wood grown in sustainable forests.
The manufacturing process conforms to the environmental
regulations of the country of origin.

For my son,
Greg

1

TWENTY-FIRST FLOOR, UNFINISHED OFFICE BLOCK, SYDNEY, AUSTRALIA

The butterfly was an Australian Painted Lady, a lost survivor of a migrating tribe. She was exhausted and beaten up, living out the last chapter of an eventful and frighteningly short life. Her wings spoke of a thousand miles of hard travel, their edges frayed and ragged.

Her youthful brilliance was long gone, the bright oranges of her wing markings bleached by sunlight to a dusty brown. Even the spectacular aquamarine eyespots of her hindwings had been scored out to an ordinary shade of grey.

Some months earlier, in the first ecstatic flights of her young life, this creature had danced among the Foxtail palms and thousand-year-old Kauri trees of the forests of Queensland, tasted the nectar of Illawarra Flame flowers and feasted on candy coloured orchids as big as your fist.

Now she was stressed and alone, trapped on the twenty-first floor of an unfinished office block high above Sydney, a dusty deathtrap devoid of liquid or plants.

It was just past seven a.m. on the 31st of December. The last day of the year. The Australian Painted Lady shrugged mortar dust from her tattered wings and beat herself against the glass in her quest for freedom and light.

2

CENTRAL BUSINESS DISTRICT, SYDNEY, AUSTRALIA

Twenty-one floors below, on the pavement outside that same office building, a seventeen-year-old Australian girl called Hannah was setting up for the day.

All she had with her was a small tin marked with the words *'Hungry. Please help'*, a filthy nylon sleeping bag . . .

And a feisty fur-ball of a mongrel tied to a grubby bit of string.

Fleabilly was the mutt's name, a cross-eyed warrior to his scruffy core. He was a pocket-sized dog, part terrier most people thought, but he punched way above his weight when it came to a fight. Hannah had seen him take on the odd Rottweiler when he was in the mood. She loved Fleabilly's pugnacious attitude and his oddball squinty look, knew he would defend her to the bitter end if necessary and that she would do the same for him.

A social worker had once asked Hannah to write a single sentence which would sum up her view of the world. Hannah chewed on a pencil for a bit then wrote:

'The more I learn about people, the more I love my dog.'

Hannah and Fleabilly had been living rough in Sydney's parks for a good few weeks, long enough for her to have learned that it was a dangerous place for a seventeen-year-old girl to be. She couldn't go home; the very thought of returning to her drunken bully of a father was too much to contemplate. Her mother was long gone and had cut all contact; even her beloved brother Todd had gone travelling to escape.

Now, Hannah put the tin on the pavement in front of her. Fleabilly was badly in need of some breakfast.

3

The security guard was Markos Dean. 'Marko' to his friends. He was twenty-two years old, filling in time with this temporary job while he waited for something better to turn up.

Marko had been waiting for something better to turn up since he flunked out of school aged fifteen.

Marko weighed in at just over ninety-five kilos and he kept himself in good shape. He did a bit of door work at some of Sydney's rougher nightclubs and he put in a few hours a week as a lifeguard when the beaches were busy.

Today he had the morning shift. From six a.m. until two p.m. this part-constructed shell of a building was Marko's domain, a towering prefabricated monolith of steel girders and polished aluminium panels.

The building should have been completed months before but the global credit crisis had spun out of nowhere and construction had ground to a halt. Money which had once flowed like water was now mysteriously unavailable. The pipes were jammed. The system froze. A new financial ice age had begun, and now no one was thinking of moving into glossy new palaces in Sydney no matter how heavenly the view of the harbour bridge.

The construction workers laid down their tools.

And Marko began his shifts.

Now, Marko took the lift up to the top floor, the twenty-fifth, from where he would start his hourly inspection tour.

4

Hannah had a lucky start to the day. Almost as soon as she put out her begging bowl a good Samaritan threw a couple of coins into the pot. 'Thanks, mate,' she called after him. 'And happy New Year.'

She scanned the street. Looking for any sign of cops. Or even her father.

Was he out looking for her? That was her biggest nightmare.

Christmas night had been the toughest of all. Curled up with Fleabilly in the back seat of a burned-out car down by the port. Faded memories of the days when her family had—after a fashion—still functioned. The days before her mother had the breakdown. The days before her father became a monster with the booze, spiralling out of a job into the blackest of depressions, then on to a three month stretch in the Long Bay Correctional Centre for the fight that gave Hannah a black eye and a chipped tooth.

Hannah had tried to defend her mother. Her father swore he would never forgive her for that.

Social services had been on her case, put her in a hostel for a few nights. But many of the other residents had drug problems and when Hannah's room mate offered her heroin she ran back to the streets.

Anything was better than *that.*

Another couple of coins hit the tin. 'Two more dollars,' she told Fleabilly, 'and we'll split a bacon sandwich.'

5

Marko took out his mobile and buzzed a call to his girlfriend Denise to relieve some of the boredom of the security patrol.

'Hey, Den. G'morning. How you doing?'

The chat continued, just mundane early morning catch up until Marko reached the twenty-first floor and took a cursory look around the empty room. Suddenly, a fluttering movement caught his eye. Something was caught in the room. Marko walked over to take a look. For a moment he thought it was a small bird, but as he got closer he realized it was a ragged looking butterfly, beating itself crazy against a window.

'Bug invasion,' he told Denise. 'That's about as exciting as it gets here, babe.'

It wasn't a phobia exactly, but if there was one thing that Marko hated more than anything else it was butterflies and moths. Something about their fat, hairy bodies just made him squirm.

'I'll call you back.' Marko cut the call.

He put on one of his leather gloves. He stepped up to the window and slammed his palm hard against the glass in an attempt to kill the butterfly. But the creature was fast, and he missed it by a couple of inches.

Instead, the impact had the most surprising effect; the glass panel popped right out of its frame and fell away from the building. Marko leaned forward in shock, watching in horror as the huge pane of glass fell towards the street below.

6

The cruise ship was the MS *Cayman Glory*, weighing in at 85,000 tonnes and cruising now towards Sydney harbour at eighteen knots. She was one of a new generation of super-de luxe vessels, fitted out to the exacting standards of a five star hotel and catering for an international clientele who like their luxury and are not afraid to pay for it.

The captain was Stian Olberg, a stout, fifty-six-year-old Norwegian who was celebrating his twenty-fifth year at sea. Olberg had brought many vessels into Sydney harbour and even though he'd never show it to his crew, he always relished the natural drama of this most spectacular of ports.

'Reduce speed. Eight knots,' Olberg told his first officer. He nodded to the radio officer, 'Raise Harbour Control.'

The radio officer switched his VHF transmitter to Channel 13: 'Harbour control. This is MS *Cayman Glory* reporting five miles south-east of pilot boarding ground. ETA twenty minutes.'

'Harbour control,' confirmed the reply. 'G'day, *Cayman Glory*. Your pilot will shortly be on board cutter and heading out, over.'

Captain Olberg felt the deck beneath his feet tremble slightly as the MS *Cayman Glory* reduced speed. He took a sip of black coffee and put on his sunglasses.

It was a fine day for cruising.

7

Another coin clinked into Hannah's begging tin. People were being extra generous today, she thought; must be the holiday mood.

Hannah could see her reflection in the window of the office building but the vision was so upsetting she had to look away. She looked a mess: the dreadlocks she had once been so proud of were matted and filthy.

'Is it just me,' she asked Fleabilly, 'or does one of us need a bath?'

He nuzzled her hand as a reply.

Hannah knew she couldn't run for ever. Living rough was awful. At night she got hassled by drunks. During the day she dodged the police who were constantly on her case.

There was an aunt up in Brisbane that she was fond of, one of the few relatives who had always given her love and support. Hannah had a feeling she might offer her a new home but how would she get there with no cash? She didn't even know how far away Brisbane was; a few hundred miles? A thousand?

It was hopeless.

'Time for breakfast,' she told Fleabilly.

An instant later she saw something flash through the air.

8

The pane of glass hit the roof of a passing truck in the street below. The impact speed was about one hundred and forty kilometres an hour. Twisting as it fell, it was precisely flat relative to the ground as it cannoned into one of the re-inforced steel frame supports that held the canvas truck-roof in shape.

The effect was a veritable explosion of glass as the huge laminated pane ripped itself into thousands of razor sharp shards. Each spun off on its own random trajectory, blitzing the road—and those using it—with a shower of potentially deadly fragments, and sending pedestrians scurrying for cover.

The noise was shocking. Hannah's little dog nearly jumped out of his skin. He shot to his feet in panic and ran blindly into the road:

'Fleabilly! Come back here!'

One blade-shaped shard embedded itself in the tyre of a speeding taxi. The driver, shocked by the sudden blowout, felt his vehicle lurch to one side.

Fleabilly was struck a glancing blow.

The impact sent him flying. He somersaulted twice, crashed hard onto the road and lay still.

Hannah was covered in cuts from the flying glass but she rushed forward and gathered Fleabilly up in her arms.

A thin trickle of blood was running from his ear.

9

Marko took the stairs at a run, four, five steps at a time, his torch and keys flying unheeded from his kit belt as he spiralled crazily fast down through the building. He was praying, praying harder than he'd done in a long time, that that lethal pane of glass hadn't already killed someone . . .

Eighth floor, sixth, second . . . What the hell had happened there? Marko's frantic mind was trying to figure out how that pane of glass had popped out of the frame. Sure, he'd hit it pretty hard, and he was a strong guy. But how come it wasn't fixed in place?

If his brain hadn't been otherwise engaged he might have worked it out: the construction team responsible for fitting the windows on the twenty-first floor had downed their tools mid-task when they'd heard they were being made redundant. They'd retired to a local bar to drown their sorrows, leaving one of the windows fixed loosely with its rubber seal but missing the grouting that would fix it securely to the frame.

A simple case of human error.

Marko hit the ground floor. He raced through the half finished corridor into the atrium and pushed his way through the revolving door into the glaring sunlight.

The traffic was at a standstill. A handful of wounded pedestrians were clutching handkerchiefs and tissues to their cuts.

Nearby he could see a scruffy looking girl with dread-locks. She was cradling a dog in her arms. A dog that was curiously still.

'You OK?' Marko asked her.

She stared at him blankly, evidently in shock.

10

The pilot vessel was a compact fifteen metre craft, a rugged vessel constructed for speed and manoeuvrability in the roughest of sea conditions. It was painted bright orange, like most pilot vessels of its type.

Ella Andersen was one of seven pilots on duty that day, a thirty-seven-year-old Sydneyite with the clear skin and glowing complexion that comes with a working life at sea.

Like most harbour pilots, Ella had considerable experience as a captain, and had for some ten years or so been responsible for cargo vessels on the Trans Pacific routes from Australia to the west coast of the States. When her two kids came along, Ella looked for a job closer to home, finally securing one of the coveted Sydney Harbour pilot jobs against stiff competition.

Now she grabbed a quick coffee from the canteen and made her way to the pilot vessel where her helmsman already had the engine running.

'Morning, Frank. What's on the list?'

'*Cayman Glory.*' Ella couldn't help a little buzz of pleasure when she heard this news. All pilots like the challenge of bringing big ships into port—and the cruisers are the biggest of all.

Ella's helmsman gave the cutter some revs and she waved to the radio operator as they headed out of the Watson's Bay pilot station and into the open sea.

11

The truck that had stopped the falling pane of glass was a seven tonne flatbed fitted with a canvas roof.

It was carrying fireworks. Almost five tonnes of fireworks to be precise.

The explosive devices were all boxed up and ready for the New Year display which would blaze above the skies of Sydney that very night.

The fireworks were the responsibility of Shaun Spencer, a twenty-three-year-old geek best described as a die-hard firework nut. He had been addicted to big bangs since seeing his first display at the age of six and from that point on all he had ever wanted was to plan, build, and choreograph bigger and bigger firework displays. He had the imagination for it, and he definitely had the passion, and the displays he designed undoubtedly had an edge over his competitors.

He was young to be leading such an event but there was no one better for the job. His work colleagues called him the 'Gunpowder Geek'—a nickname he was curiously proud of.

Now Shaun was moving to the back of the truck with his driver and de-rigging the rope ties so they could have a good look at the interior. The falling glass had hit the truck with an almighty smash. What concerned him now was this question: had any of his precious fireworks been damaged? Certainly the canvas roof had been lacerated by many pieces of glass.

'What do you think?' he asked the driver.

'Better safe than sorry.' The two men jumped up onto the back of the truck and began to survey the boxes for damage.

12

Marko was walking around the street, trying to pick up the bigger pieces of glass, a terrible feeling of guilt engulfing him. A tall blond man turned up on a motorbike and Marko heard him say he was a doctor; he opened up his pannier and brought out a first aid kit to help the wounded.

A traffic cop had reached the scene; he was trying to make some sense of what had happened. A TV crew rolled up from a local news channel and began to film.

Marko could have walked away from it all. He could have kept his mouth shut, denied all knowledge of the falling glass. After all, he figured, the pane had been so poorly fixed that it might have been dislodged by the wind.

But that wasn't Marko's style. He was an honest guy, so that when a cop came over to him and asked 'Any idea what happened here?' Marko told him the truth.

'You are one lucky guy,' the cop told Marko as he looked up at the building. 'Piece of glass that size falling all that way and no fatalities.'

Marko heard a sobbing noise; he looked round. He saw that same girl, the one with the dreadlocks, standing in shock with the motionless body of that small dog still in her arms. She didn't seem to have moved, was just standing there crying with this utterly destroyed look on her face.

'I recognize that girl,' the cop said. 'Her photo's on our website. I'm going to talk to her.'

'I think her dog just got killed,' Marko blurted out. 'Don't you think you should wait a—'

But the cop was already moving towards Hannah.

13

The pilot cutter was still heading for the *Cayman Glory* when Ella remembered the letter that had arrived at home that morning.

Air mail from Liberia in West Africa. News from her sister Gwen, now working as a missionary.

She opened the blue envelope by sliding her thumbnail along the seam. Inside was a handwritten letter and a photograph. She tucked the letter away to read when she had more time.

The picture showed her sister Gwen. She was standing, smiling, in front of a small jungle chapel with a group of children posing excitedly with her.

The image gave Ella mixed feelings. She knew that Gwen was happy in her new role, but she was also aware that civil war had flared up in Liberia and that her sister's life could be in danger.

Ella and her sister had been raised in the hothouse environment of an ultra religious family. Their father had been a strict Catholic, and the guilt of 'renouncing God' had stayed with Ella even into her adult life. The mere sight of a church, or an image of Christ on the cross was enough, for Ella, to provoke memories of a chronically unhappy childhood.

Gwen had kept her faith—even studying at a religious college for a while. Later she had left for West Africa and a job as chief coordinator for a Christian Sisterhood.

Ella sighed. She missed her sister more every day. 'Ten minutes,' the helmsman told her. Ella put the photograph in her pocket and reached for her immersion suit.

14

Fleabilly.

Dead.

Hannah was used to the world turning against her. But this was something else . . .

She was so stunned that she hardly felt the cop's hand on her arm. 'I know who you are,' he told her firmly, 'and I want you to stay right here. As soon as I've sorted out this mess I'm taking you to the station.'

He walked away from Hannah and that was when she saw the motorbike. The Honda Transalp standing on the pavement with the back pannier open and the engine still running.

She knew she could ride it, she'd been taught by her brother Todd and could handle even the biggest dirt bikes on rough terrain.

Something inside her snapped.

A tidal wave of grief and fury overwhelmed her. Fleabilly's death had pushed her right over the edge.

Hannah placed Fleabilly's body in the back pannier, leapt onto the machine and kicked it into gear. She gave it plenty on the throttle and raced at breakneck speed down the street. The owner of the bike shouted out—a cry of shock—as he realized his machine was being driven off. The cop tried to grab her, but Hannah swerved around him and made it out of the melee.

She felt the wind rip through her hair as the bike

accelerated with a satisfying surge of power. The tears were still rolling but the moment felt right.

She had to find a place to say goodbye to Fleabilly. Then it was time to get out of town.

15

Susannah Gately was doing her normal morning thing when the telephone rang: trying to feed and dress her two pre-school kids while they screamed, fought, kicked and generally created toddler mayhem.

Susannah frowned. The phone had ID caller function and she didn't recognize the number. A slight tremor of nerves hit her. Nobody likes early morning calls from unknown numbers. 'Hello?'

'It's me.' Susannah could immediately detect the abnormal tone of her husband's voice. The motorbike flashed in her mind. Had he had an accident?

'Don't worry. I'm fine. But get this,' her husband told her, 'some crazy kid just stole the Transalp.'

'*What?*'

'Yeah, I stopped to help out at this accident and I left the engine running. And it's worse . . . all my stuff is in the pannier, the laptop with my patient records, the wallet, the works. I just borrowed this phone from a guy here. We have to cancel the credit cards . . . tell the phone company to block the calls on the mobile.'

'OK, Ash, I'll do it as fast as I can.'

'Honey, one more thing. I backed up my patient records onto a memory stick. It's on my desk. Can you bring it down to town for me? I'll need them today at the hospital.'

Susannah drew a sharp breath. She flashed a glance at the clock. Their house was right out in the forested fringes of the city. The round trip to town would take her a good hour and she was supposed to get their two toddlers to their nursery school by ten a.m.

'OK, Ash. Tell me where you are.' She grabbed a pen.

16

Ella picked up her binoculars and focused with a deft twist of her fingers.

There, proudly profiled against an azure sky she could see in precise detail the graceful outline of the MS *Cayman Glory* arriving at the pilot boarding zone. It was right on time; precisely on the edge of the area on the charts known as Port Area Alpha.

'She's a beauty,' Ella commented.

She sipped her coffee again, relishing the kick of the caffeine through the sweet haze of sugar as the little pilot vessel pitched through the rolling trans-Pacific swell.

It wasn't a big sea, just a two to three metre rolling carpet of waves, but it was enough to send the shallow-keeled little vessel pitching nose first. That wouldn't worry Ella, she'd never had a moment's nausea in five years as a pilot.

A short time later they came up alongside the huge cruiser. It was making eight knots, as requested, to make the boarding easier. Ella zipped up her immersion suit and stepped out onto the tiny foredeck of the vessel as her helmsman skilfully brought the speed up to match the precise headway of the cruiser.

Some thirty metres above her position, on the bridge, Captain Olberg was looking down on the procedure with a keen eye. He could see the pilot vessel was fitted with heavy duty fenders but the swell was enough to throw the tiny craft against his shiny white hull with a healthy smack.

Captain Olberg didn't want a single scratch on his beloved vessel.

17

Hannah was parked up in a derelict area of wasteground right next to the main M5 motorway out of Sydney.

She was digging a grave for Fleabilly, tears of misery and disbelief still running down her cheeks. The tool for the task was far from ideal, a broken metal fence post she had pulled from a pile of scrap.

It was tough work but her anger gave her strength, stabbing manically at the ground with the pole and scooping out the stony soil with her hands. Finally she created a hole that was big enough and she gently laid the body of Fleabilly into it.

'We never did get that bacon sandwich,' she said quietly. 'So long, buddy.'

She re-filled the little grave with dirt and pressed it down firmly with her boots.

She returned to the motorbike and, for the first time, noticed that some of the owner's possessions were still in the pannier. There was a wallet, stitched in expensive leather. Hannah opened it up with shaking fingers. Just over four hundred dollars. Next was a laptop, then she found the bike rider's mobile.

Hannah knew that the owner of these possessions would even now be calling to block his cards, de-activate the phone. But if she was fast she might be able to talk to her brother. Hannah selected the call facility, dialling the number from memory.

She heard the call tone ringing five times before her brother's surprised voice came onto the line. 'Hello?'

'G'day, Todd,' Hannah said, trying to bite back the tears, 'just thought you might like to hear from your little sister.'

18

At that moment, in the main atrium of the *Cayman Glory*, a twenty-two-year-old carpenter by the name of Bruce Tiler was opening up his tool kit in readiness for a special task.

In front of him was the huge nativity scene that had been built on board to celebrate Christmas in Fiji some six days earlier.

This festive extravaganza was, like everything on the *Cayman Glory*, gaudy, colourful, and huge. There was a full-sized wooden manger, life-sized fibreglass figurines of the holy family, the three wise men, and a pair of luxuriously winged angels for good measure. Every detail had been carefully considered, right down to the full-sized plastic donkey and the straw sprinkled around the manger. It was a fitting centrepiece for the spectacular atrium and Captain Olberg himself had congratulated Bruce on a job well done.

Now, with the Christmas festivities over and the cruise coming to an end, the nativity scene was to be dismantled and returned to a storage facility on dry land.

Bruce took his screwdriver out of the toolbox and began the job. Nearby was a huge plasma screen television. The breakfast news was running; one of Sydney's twenty-four hour channels feeding into the atrium. Bruce kept a casual eye on the screen as he began to dismantle the nativity scene.

Then he saw a face he recognized.

Marko! An old school mate. Dressed in a security guard uniform and running around the street like a headless chicken. Bruce had to smile. What on earth had old Marko done to get himself on the news?

19

Susannah slammed down the telephone.

Cancelling Ash's credit cards had been an unwelcome hassle but now it was done. His mobile operators had also promised to cut the line as 'soon as possible'—whatever that meant.

In the meantime, one of her kids had soiled his nappy. The other, taking advantage of his mother's distraction, had spread most of the contents of a box of choco crispies all over the sitting room floor then stamped it into a sort of powdery goo.

Susannah grabbed hold of the kids. Out to the car, a Subaru 4x4. Kids in the back. Strapped into their car seats. More tears and tantrums. Heck. Ash's memory stick. In all the rush she had almost set out without it.

Susannah rushed back inside to retrieve the pen drive. She found it quickly and was just leaving when she saw the mug of coffee sitting on the sideboard. Thanks to Ash's call she hadn't had a chance to touch it.

She decided to drink it in the car.

Out to the vehicle. A last minute drama: kid number two had managed to drop his dummy out of the car. Susannah put the mug of coffee on the roof of the Subaru as she bent to search for it.

Dummy found. Smiles all round. Susannah closed the kids' doors, climbed into the driver's seat and turned the ignition.

She pulled out of the driveway and turned right towards Sydney on the forest road. The mug of coffee was still sitting, completely forgotten, on the roof of the Subaru.

20

It was late afternoon in the Amazon. Todd Williams had been sleeping when the vibration of his mobile against his skin woke him up. In fact the backpacker had been out for the count after three exhausting days of hard travelling on the rickety old rural buses which had brought him to this tributary of the great river.

Now, as he took the call, he was curled up on the open wooden deck of a decrepit old river steamer, his head resting on his rucksack to prevent it getting stolen. He was fortunate, at that precise moment, to be close to a mobile transmitter—the cellphone tower at the remote river settlement of Porto Velho.

'G'day, Todd. Just thought you might like to hear from your little sister.'

Hannah! Todd had been longing for news from his sister. Two weeks previously, in Manaus, he had picked up an email from his father telling him that Hannah had left home and was living rough on the streets of Sydney. Ever since then he had been waiting anxiously for a call which would tell him his vulnerable sister was OK.

'Hey! That's great to hear from you! Did you get my email?'

'Your what? I can hardly . . . the line's breaking up . . . '

'Not surprising. I'm halfway up a river in the Amazon.'

A babble of unintelligible static came back at him. Todd

tried to decipher his sister's words but the sound of conversation around him was intense and the mobile signal was breaking up. 'Hang on, sis. Let me see if I can get a better signal.'

But suddenly the line faded and died.

21

Captain Olberg needn't have worried about the paintwork of the *Cayman Glory*. The powerful little pilot vessel was in expert hands and Ella Andersen had gone through the hair-raising routine of transferring onto 'Jacob's ladders' many hundreds of times.

Ella judged the swell just right, transferring her weight to the ladder at the top of the wave and swarming up the rungs as her helmsman peeled away to head back to port.

Ella was met by the officer of the watch and shown to the lift which would take them to deck level four. From there they would have to cross the atrium to get to the private, crew only, lifts rising to the bridge.

'Have you been on board before?' the officer asked her as they entered the enormous atrium.

'No. Not this vessel,' she said, pausing for a moment in awe at the sheer audacious scale of the thing. 'But I have to admit it's quite a sight!'

Ella wasn't being polite for the sake of it. The *Cayman Glory* atrium really *was* something else with its impressive glass roof and rows of luxury shops. She could see scores of passengers hunting desperately for last minute gifts— there was just an hour or so of their cruise left to go.

A few steps ahead, Ella could see a man working on a huge nativity scene. He seemed to be in the middle of taking it to pieces. The sight gave her a nervous twist in her gut; life-sized figurines of angels and other holy figures had always given her the spooks.

She picked up her pace to hurry past.

22

Terry Alton was a Sydney motorbike cop on routine highway patrol; he was riding a 1000cc BMW bike, a machine capable of catching even the fastest Porsche or Ferrari in a chase.

From his high vantage point on a motorway flyover he saw a solitary motorbike on the wasteground below. A girl was standing next to it, tapping numbers into a mobile.

Fifteen years on patrol gives a cop a nose for something that doesn't look right, and Terry knew right away that he would have to go down and investigate this girl. Apart from anything else she had no helmet, which was odd. And illegal.

At the first possible exit, Terry indicated and pulled off the freeway. He parked up in a position where he could observe her clandestinely and also make a radio call back to base: 'Five nine four. Five nine four. You got any reports of a girl on a stolen bike?'

'Roger your message, five nine four. Please hold.'

Terry watched as the girl put the mobile to her ear. Then the radio buzzed back into life:

'That's an affirmative. Honda Transalp reported stolen earlier in the central business district. Suspect young girl with dreadlocks. No helmet.'

'Roger. I'm on wasteground beneath junction five and I have her visual. Going to apprehend now.'

Terry put the radio handset back in its holder and kicked the BMW into first gear. He drove out onto the wasteground, heading directly for the girl.

23

In the atrium of the *Cayman Glory*, Bruce the carpenter was completely distracted from his job of dismantling the ship's Christmas nativity scene. He was still trying to work out why his old mate Marko was on the TV.

He was glued to the screen. There was Marko again. It was definitely him, but what exactly had happened? It looked like some sort of traffic incident. Bruce moved a little closer to the screen, trying to hear the news reporter's voice. At that precise instant he was supporting the weight of the figure of the Virgin Mary, an almost life-sized resin sculpture which weighed in at a hefty thirty or so kilos.

He still couldn't hear the commentary. He balanced the figurine on the edge of the stage which supported the nativity scene, holding it in position with one hand as he stretched for the plasma screen and the small buttons on the side panel which would allow him to boost up the volume.

Then the figurine slipped. And fell.

Bruce just had time to yell:

'Watch out!'

24

As soon as she saw the police motorbike approaching, Hannah stuffed the mobile into her pocket. She leapt onto the motorbike and rode off across the wasteground at high speed. Her feet were kicking through the gears as she bumped and jolted across the ditches and ruts of the hard-baked ground. She risked a look back. The cop was riding just as hard, clearly determined not to lose her.

The guy knew what he was doing on rough terrain.

Fifty kilometres an hour. Hannah was catching air as the motorbike shot across a series of undulations where a dried-out river bed crossed the trail.

Hannah reached the freeway access point. She hit the roundabout at sixty, seventy kilometres an hour, as fast as she dared without going into a potentially deadly slide. The cop was gaining on her, his 1000cc engine giving him twice as much power as her smaller Honda.

She was taking crazy risks but no way was Hannah going to be caught. The four hundred dollars had sparked an idea in her head. She could use it to get to Brisbane.

See if that aunt would give her a fresh start.

Hannah had a sudden crazy impulse. She turned the wrong way up the access ramp. Going *against* the traffic. Surely the cop would never dare to follow?

Adrenaline pumping, she gave the machine more gas, the wind rushing in her ears as her hair streamed out behind her.

25

Ella saw the statue falling. She acted on impulse, throwing herself forward to catch it.

She did catch the resin statue but it was far heavier than it had looked and the weight caused her to slam to the floor with the figurine of the Virgin Mary still held in her arms. Onlooking passengers gasped as they saw the incident. Bruce the carpenter placed his hands over his eyes in disgust at his own clumsiness.

Then Ella felt the pain in her hands.

Pulling them free from the statue she saw to her amazement that both her palms had been punctured by something sharp. Brilliant red beads of blood were seeping from the strangely round holes in her flesh.

'You all right, love?' The carpenter was right by her—helping her to her feet.

'Yeah. I'm OK.'

Ella took a closer look at the statue and could see straight away what had caused the two circular wounds. The back of the resin structure had two long threaded bolts placed there to enable it to be fixed to the wall of the nativity display.

The engineer who had fashioned them had seen no need to file the ends smooth. They were razor sharp. Ella took out a handkerchief and wiped blood from both her palms.

'You're hurt,' the carpenter observed. 'Do you want me to take you to the sickbay?'

'No, no,' Ella told him hastily—she knew that the captain would be waiting for her up on the bridge.

The matter of bringing the *Cayman Glory* safely into dock was infinitely more important than a silly old superficial flesh wound . . . or two.

26

Susannah drove east on the forest road towards Sydney. The kids were still squabbling in the back of the Subaru and she put a CD into the player in hope of shutting them up.

'Sing along, kids!' she told them. And they did. Well they gurgled at least:

The wheels on the bus go round and round
round and round, round and round.
The wheels on the bus go round and round,
all through the town

The city skyline was visible some ten miles distant. Susannah thought of her husband stranded there without money, transport, or phone and she hoped she would arrive quickly for him.

She reached a point in the road where there was a tight bend.

She took the curve at fifty-six kilometres an hour.

It was a little faster than she would normally have risked but the vehicle was a four-wheel drive model and it gripped the surface of the road with ease.

Susannah and her children made it round the curve without a problem.

The china coffee mug on the roof, however, slid off and crashed onto the tarmac on the opposite side of the road.

It broke instantly into three large pieces.

Susannah drove on towards Sydney, unaware of the incident.

27

Hannah was racing down the freeway as oncoming traffic took drastic action to avoid her. Horns blazed, lights flared in warning.

The motorbike missed a truck by a whisker, passing so close that she could feel the rush of air. One of her mirrors impacted against the side of the vehicle with a resounding crack.

Seven years' bad luck, Hannah thought with a shrug as she gave the bike more revs. She felt as if she was in a computer game, so thrilling was this insane race up the wrong side of the freeway.

The thought that someone could get hurt was the last thing on her mind. It just didn't feel that real.

She dodged a car which was heading right for her, the driver leaving a trail of smoke on the freeway as he hit the brakes hard.

In her remaining side mirror she could see the cop was still following her, weaving cautiously through the traffic which was now virtually at a standstill.

'You crazy idiot!' A smartly dressed commuter wound down the window of his car to shout the abuse.

'Yeah, crazy and proud of it!' Hannah yelled back, then steered onto the hard shoulder where she could pick up more speed.

The motorbike cop had put on his siren. The aggressive two-tone was ripping through the air and his headlights were on full beam, dazzling her when she checked the mirror.

'I'll lose you,' she whispered under her breath.

28

Shaun was still stuck in the central business district checking out the boxes of fireworks in the back of the truck.

'Look at that.' The driver pointed to a number of jagged holes in the roof of the truck. 'That glass has ripped right through the canvas.' He poked his hand through one of the holes to illustrate the point.

'Lucky we sealed the boxes so well,' Shaun said as he checked a few more of the precious cartons for damage. But a moment later they were interrupted by a gruff voice from the road. It was a traffic cop, trying to shift the traffic jam.

'I need you to get this truck moving,' the cop told them, 'we've got a tailback halfway across the city.'

'OK. Whatever you say.'

Shaun and the driver abandoned their visual check of the precious cargo and jumped down off the tailgate to get back in the cab.

'Doesn't look like there's anything to worry about,' Shaun said.

Pressured by the traffic cop, Shaun hadn't had time to check right at the back of the loadbay of the truck. That was why he hadn't seen box number forty-three, where a fifteen centimetre long dagger-shaped shard of spinning glass had punched its way through the cardboard and embedded itself deeply in one of the biggest of the firework shells, a monster maroon containing almost a pound of flash powder and almost as much again of titanium.

The driver fired up the engine and put the truck into gear. 'Next stop, Harbour Bridge.'

29

Hannah took the next exit, performing a neat slalom through the oncoming vehicles and racing across a railway line. A cargo train was not far off, trundling down the tracks at a leisurely speed and for a moment she thought the cop might not make it across in front of it.

But he cleared the tracks with a few seconds to spare.

Hannah was now passing through the outskirts of town, one of the rich areas with impressive villas and mansions dotted around forested hills. She took a winding road heading up at maximum speed, the Transalp shuddering as she asked the engine for every last ounce of power.

But still the cop was coming after her.

She saw a dirt trail heading off into the bush. Thought about it. Too obvious. He'd be able to follow her tracks in the dust.

Better to stay on the blacktop, she decided, and just drive like crazy until she had a chance to lose him.

She piled on the revs. Bugs beating against her eyes. Now everything was forest. The trees passing in a blur of blue bark and green foliage. Then came the corner. A sign warning that it was a sharp one.

Maximum speed forty kilometres an hour.

Hannah came into the corner at just over seventy kilometres an hour. She knew she'd have to shift her weight right over to enable the bike to take the bend successfully.

It was a racing stance; she was driving on the limit. Then she saw the three pieces of broken china mug lying in the road right on the crux of the bend.

30

'You really should clean those wounds,' the officer told her as he examined the two puncture marks on Ella's hands.

Ella stared at the two bloody holes. They were starting to hurt like hell.

'That was a weird accident,' the officer said with a nervous laugh. Ella wished he would keep silent. The wounds were not so deep. The few drops of blood were soaked up by her handkerchief . . .

Later she would get a couple of Band-Aids and that would be the end of it.

As she stood in the lift with the ship's officer, Ella had to make a conscious effort to compose herself. The incident with the religious figurine had definitely shaken her up— and not just physically.

It really *had* been a bizarre accident, coming out of the blue in a place which seemed so ordered and safe. The workman had been distracted by the television, Ella surmised, and she wondered briefly what could have been so fascinating to him.

Just for a moment, as the lift doors were closing, Ella caught sight of the statue—now safely lying on the floor where it could do no more harm. The virgin seemed to be looking right at her. Ella shivered. Then the lift doors swiped shut with an electronic hiss.

Within a couple of minutes the pilot was ushered onto the bridge. 'Welcome aboard,' Captain Olberg greeted her. 'Want a coffee?'

'No thank you, Captain,' Ella managed to say. She managed to keep the shake out of her voice. 'Now, let's get to work, shall we? We have to get this vessel safely docked.'

31

The Transalp front tyre hit the largest of the fragments of china mug.

The blow-out was instant.

Hannah jerked the front wheel to her left in a reflex movement which put the machine into an immediate slide. Her left flank hit the tarmac with a fleshy thud, the motorbike spinning once, then twice, as it crashed onto the verge. Hannah slid on her side, away from the bike, protecting her head with her hands.

Hannah stood, panting hard with the surprise of the crash. She looked down at her thighs, swearing as she saw just how little denim fabric was left on her left leg. The slide on the gravel had eroded almost all of the tough material away, revealing a large expanse of raw flesh which was scoured and bleeding.

Hannah winced as the first wave of pain hit her.

The cop was pulling up, killing the engine on his BMW and putting it on its stand.

'You OK?' he asked Hannah.

Hannah took one look at him then retreated into the forest behind her.

'Hey! You're hurt!' the cop called. 'You need to get some attention.'

Hannah began to run, down into a forested canyon.

After a few moments she heard the heavy footsteps of the cop following her.

32

Todd stared at his mobile in frustration, willing it to ring again. The river boat was chugging ever further away from the little town of Porto Velho and he knew the signal would be getting weaker with every passing minute.

The call from his sister had been brief and entirely unsatisfactory and now almost ten minutes had passed and she hadn't rung back. That was typical of Hannah, Todd fumed, she always had been flaky.

He resolved to call her with the automatic redial facility but the single blip of signal on the mobile screen was not exactly a good sign. And his battery was almost flat. Maybe if he got a bit higher on the boat? The signal might be stronger.

Todd pushed his way through the crowded deck, trying not to squash the sleeping passengers and stepping delicately around baskets of pungent dried fish and trussed up chickens.

As soon as he reached the gangway he quickly climbed the wooden steps up towards the captain's cabin and saw to his satisfaction that the single blip on his phone had strengthened to two. Now he'd be able to have a decent conversation with his little sister. The captain was too busy navigating up the river to throw this intruder back onto the deck where he belonged.

He selected the recall button on his mobile and it

automatically called back to the number Hannah had just reached him from.

A few seconds later he could hear the ringing tone of the phone. It rang ten, fifteen, twenty times, then terminated in a loud click. 'Hannah? Can you hear me?' There was no one listening. The line was dead. Todd muttered an oath. Then he dialled again. Then he saw that the battery alert was flashing.

33

A few kilometres upstream from Todd's position a small cabin stood alone on a sweeping bend of the river.

It was a modest dwelling, made from roughly cut planks with a shaggy thatch of fronds for a roof. Supporting the whole structure were four blocks of wood, raising the cabin above the ground in the vain hope of escape from the cockroaches, scorpions, and rats which also sought to call this place home.

One family lived in this place. They were poor but they were independent and tough: typical *caboclos*—mixed race forest settlers who inherited the hard work ethic of their Amerindian and European forefathers.

The man of the house was Vicenzo; at that moment he was away in the jungle looking for game with his two hunting dogs. He had been gone for three days and the family knew he would not be back until he had a good sized monkey, or perhaps a tapir, to feed his family.

What Vicenzo could not know was that his wife Eva had been taken sick soon after his departure. She was pregnant and even though the baby was not due, the labour pains had started and a great fever had overcome her.

If she didn't get medical attention soon then her life— and the life of her unborn child—would certainly be in danger.

The only one who could help her now was her fourteen-year-old daughter Isabella.

34

Ella couldn't believe how much blood she was losing from those wounds to her hands. No matter how hard she pressed the handkerchief into her fists, she just couldn't stop the bleeding.

So she thrust her hands into her pockets in the hope that no one would notice her discomfort.

A few minutes passed as the *Cayman Glory* headed for the harbour. All was proceeding smoothly but Ella could feel blood trickling down her fingers.

When she extracted her hand from the pocket she realized that her sister's photograph was in there. She pulled out the photo, cursing as she saw that it was covered in blood.

First the injury. Now the bloodstains all over her sister's photograph.

She tried to wipe the photograph clean but succeeded only in smearing more blood over her sister's face. Suddenly Ella felt the most curious sensation of dread overcoming her. The pace of her breathing increased dramatically. She clutched the back of a chair next to the chart table.

'Are you all right?' the captain asked her.

'Yeah, just some sort of virus I guess . . . '

Ella realized she was having some sort of panic attack . . . something that had never happened to her before.

'I'll be back in a couple of minutes,' she told the crew.

They nodded understandingly. There was still about fifteen minutes to go before the ship would be entering the harbour so she had plenty of time.

As soon as she had left the bridge Ella punched on her mobile. The bloodied photo had seemed to be a *warning*.

She had to check that Gwen was OK.

35

The incident with the falling glass had delayed Shaun's truck full of fireworks by almost an hour.

The schedule for rigging the many thousands of fireworks onto the Sydney Harbour Bridge was already a tight one but now it was super tight.

Shaun felt himself fuming as they hit heavy traffic downtown. The holiday traffic was in full flow. His carefully made plans to squeeze through Sydney before the bulk of the morning jams had been foiled by a freak accident and he was not the least happy about it.

The hand-made devices carefully packed into wooden cases behind him were much more than a source of entertainment to Shaun.

They were his babies. And he loved every single one.

At that moment Shaun's mobile rang. A call he had been expecting from a local FM radio station keen to find out about the pyrotechnic show to come.

'Is that Shaun?' A woman's voice—the producer. 'We're putting you through live to the show now. Hold the line.'

'OK.'

Shaun heard the tonsil rattling bass tones of one of Sydney's best known Radio Jocks. 'In just a couple of minutes we'll be talking to the man responsible for tonight's firework spectacular. That's right after Kylie who is, as ever, "Spinning Around" . . . '

Shaun knew he had to brighten himself up for this, force

the stress out of his voice in an attempt to sound cool, calm, and collected. He took a swig of water to loosen his throat and waited to go live to the good people of Sydney.

36

Fourteen-year-old Isabella was out collecting berries in the forest when she heard her mother scream out in pain. It was a terrible sound—far worse than the cries that had come before. She dropped her basket and ran for home, pushing quickly through the dense undergrowth.

Isabella ran through the garden, taking care not to step on the straggly bean plants and a few manioc roots that struggled to grow there.

She entered the cabin and placed her hand on her mother's brow, feeling immediately that she was still feverish. The cotton hammock was soaked with sweat and her normally sweet breath was sour from the vomiting.

'It is worse,' her mother whispered, her lips trembling slightly as a spasm coursed through her pelvis. 'The baby wants to come but I can't do any more . . . ' Her mother looked at her watch. It was well past five o'clock in the afternoon and there was less than an hour and a half of daylight left.

'I cannot wait any longer. You have to go to Porto Velho. Get the doctor to come.'

These were the words that Isabella had been dreading. To get to the nearest town the fourteen-year-old girl would have to paddle alone down the Rio Jari in a canoe that was designed to be handled by a fully grown man. There were currents that could tip her over in a moment and—just above the outpost settlement of Porto Velho, there was a section of whitewater rapids which even the hardiest *caboclos* avoided if they possibly could.

'Mama . . . I cannot . . . The river.'

Isabella's mother looked at her through a haze of tears. 'Please, Isabella. I cannot survive another night. You have to try.'

37

CARGO LOADING ZONE: SYDNEY INTERNATIONAL AIRPORT

With the *Cayman Glory* coming into Sydney harbour for a swift turn around, a whole army of suppliers were getting ready to service the ship.

One of them was Trinny Davis, a thirty-year-old divorcée originally from Cairns who was the proud owner-operator of a refrigerated truck.

Her contract, one of many she had to complete that day, was to pick up a consignment of live lobsters at Sydney International airport and deliver them to the *Cayman Glory*.

The lobsters were from New England in the USA. They had been flown in from Maine that morning and kept in a cold storage unit in the cargo area of the airport waiting to be picked up. In total there were five tonnes of the creatures with a commercial value of some twenty thousand dollars. They were packed in special Styrofoam shipping containers designed to maintain the perfect level of humidity (not less than ninety-five per cent so that their gills remain moist) and temperature (anything between thirty-two degrees and forty degrees Fahrenheit is acceptable) to keep the creatures alive.

First class cruise ship passengers such as those on the *Cayman Glory* like their lobster fresh. Frozen lobster just doesn't taste *quite* so good.

'Picking up for the *Cayman Glory*,' she told the security guard at the entrance to the airport cargo area.

'Go right through.'

Trinny parked up outside the main cargo transit warehouse and handed the paperwork to the cargo loadmaster. He retreated to his office to check the computer and she helped herself to a plastic cup of chilled water from a dispenser while she waited for him to return.

38

Shaun's slot on the show came up after a short delay.

'Talking about tonight's celebrations,' the radio jock intoned, 'I'm joined now live by Shaun Spencer, the big boss of tonight's big bang. What can we expect from this year's firework display, Shaun?'

'Well. Five tonnes of fireworks is an awful lot of bang.' Shaun gave his characteristic nervous laugh. 'It could easily blow the roof off the Sydney Opera House, given the right circumstances, of course.'

'Heck, Shaun,' the radio jock whistled, 'hope you got a long match to light all that lot.'

'It's all electronic,' the Gunpowder Geek replied. 'The whole show gets fired up and timed from pressing a single button.'

'Awesome. Do you ever get frightened that you're going to press that switch and nothing's going to happen . . . ? That's what would keep me awake at night!'

Shaun laughed. 'I don't worry about that,' he said. 'Rain's the only thing that can give us a bit of a headache . . . '

'And as I understand it, the whole thing is hand made, is that right? How long does it take you to put it together?'

'About six months to plan it on paper,' Shaun told him, 'then we have twenty people working on the manufacture for the rest of the year.'

'So it's the same as painting the bridge, right?' the radio jock laughed. 'As soon as you finish tonight's show you'll be starting off the next one?'

'That's about it,' Shaun agreed. Just a few hundred metres ahead, Shaun could see the access road leading up to the Harbour Bridge.

39

Isabella ran down the small track to the little sandy beach where the family canoe was pulled up out of the water. The vessel was a simple dug-out, a rough and ready piece of work which her father had made himself. Basically he had hacked at a section of Itauba trunk with an axe until he had something that vaguely resembled a boat.

Isabella knew she should push the canoe onto the water and start straight away but first she scanned the water, her heart beating with a crazy hope, praying that she would see the reassuring sight of a trading vessel or a motor launch coming up from the nearest town.

Nothing.

The river was red with silt; recent rainfall in the distant highlands had swollen it to the highest level Isabella had ever seen. She had always feared the water, harboured secret terrors of the anacondas, the electric rays, and other unknown predators that lurked beneath these sinuous waters.

Another scream of pain came from the hut.

Isabella untied the canoe from its mooring and climbed in. She took up the paddle and propelled the canoe with a tentative stroke into the flow of the river.

The current was swift and strong. Isabella took a deep breath and gritted her teeth as she dipped the paddle once again into the water. The river was so huge. She had never felt so small and fragile in her life.

But she had to go through with this. If she could survive the rapids then her mother and her unborn child might be saved.

FOREST ROAD, WEST SYDNEY SUBURBS, AUSTRALIA

The exhaust pipe on the Transalp was burning almost red hot. Hannah had been pushing the engine so hard that the metal was easily capable of igniting anything flammable which came into contact.

A single stem of grass was leaning against the fallen bike where it lay in the verge. Soon it was smouldering, then it flickered into a flame.

The forest was tinder dry. Nine months of savage drought had seen just five or six paltry millimetres of rain in New South Wales. The trees were starved of moisture, their leaves desiccated and as brittle as parchment.

The day was windy, a consistent ten to fifteen kilometre an hour breeze from the west. A hot, dry wind.

Perfect conditions for a raging forest fire.

It took approximately four minutes for the single stem of burning grass to ignite every strand on the verge. The flames flared up, licking eagerly at the lowest branches of the eucalyptus, alpine ash and acacia trees which thrived in this place. The light hissing sound of the grass fire took on a new tone as branches and leaves crackled and snapped above the flames.

Seconds later they were ablaze, the fire feeding greedily on the highly flammable eucalyptus oil and jumping from one tree crown to the next as the wind fanned the flames.

Now the forest was well alight. Birds and other forest

creatures scented the air, alarmed as they smelt the acrid smoke drifting across the valley.

Soon they would be fleeing for their lives. And so would Hannah and the cop.

41

MISSION OF THE SISTERS OF CHRIST, LIBERIA, WEST AFRICA

Ella's sister Gwen was fast asleep in her simple room at the mission school in West Africa when the satellite phone rang. It was almost ten p.m. local time.

Gwen hated having the satellite phone close to her every moment of the day and night but the heads of her religious order had insisted on it. The region of West Africa in which Gwen was working had recently erupted in a series of violent clashes between government troops and renegade rebels. Many missions had been attacked and ransacked. Gwen herself had been threatened and verbally abused in the market of the nearest town.

'Ella?' Gwen felt a pang of homesickness as she heard her sister's voice for the first time in several months. Leaving Sydney and all the family behind had been a tough price to pay for her Christian calling but Gwen knew that was the path she had to follow.

'I just had to check you're OK.'

'I'm hanging on in there, Ella.'

'Just something weird happened to me just now and it gave me the shivers. I thought it might mean . . . you were in danger.'

'Something weird? Like what?'

Ella related the story of the falling Virgin Mary to her sister. 'I don't know, Gwen,' she continued. 'Now I have these wounds on my hands. It was . . . it was like a sign, I don't know. Like something is going to happen. I have no idea what . . . but for some reason I'm scared.'

Gwen suddenly tensed up. There was a noise. From the jungle outside. It sounded like a man's cough—hurriedly stifled. 'Hold the line a moment, sis.' Gwen pulled back the curtain and stared out into the night.

42

THE LOTUS MONASTERY, YANGON, MYANMAR, SOUTH-EAST ASIA

At that moment, seventeen thousand kilometres to the east, in the capital city of Myanmar, an alarm bell went off at the stroke of 5 a.m. local time.

Wai Yan—a sixteen-year-old monk—switched off the device and sleepily climbed out of his bed.

Wai Yan was a Buddhist; he had been a novice monk in the Sangha community since taking his first vows at the age of six. Seen from a western perspective, his life might have seemed unbearably dull. The prayers alone took up six hours a day and personal possessions were frowned upon.

But sports were encouraged and that was good news for Wai Yan because his hours kicking a ball around on the monastery's dusty little makeshift pitch were some of the happiest of his life. He was a useful winger, fast and a good crosser of the ball, but he was also a fanatical supporter. And, like millions of other football nuts in Asia, Manchester United was his team.

Manchester United. The Red Devils. Wai Yan worshipped them, following their every match on his (illegal) little short-wave radio and watching them on television when he got a chance. On the walls of his little cell faded magazine photos of Man U legends like Ryan Giggs, Wayne Rooney, and David Beckham took pride of place. When one of the lamas was due to make an inspection he would cover the pictures with a poster of Buddha.

Today, Wai Yan had been asked to attend a demonstration in the People's Park; he was excited by the prospect, keen to take his place amongst the thousands of other monks and intellectuals.

He slipped his little short-wave radio into his backpack. The Champions League draws for the final sixteen knock-out stage would be announced later that day and there was no way he wanted to miss *that*.

43

Todd's mobile battery had died on him but that didn't mean he was going to give up. He knew this might be his only chance for weeks to speak to his sister and he wondered if there was power on board the boat to get a quick charge up. He rapped on the window of the captain's little cabin, thinking—not for the first time—what a good decision it had been to spend a year learning the local language before the journey.

'I need to charge my mobile,' Todd told the captain as he waved his mobile in the air.

'What do you think this is?' the captain shouted back with a drunken and sarcastic smile. 'A five star hotel?'

'You've got an engine,' Todd insisted, 'you must have electricity.'

'They might be able to fix you up in the engine room,' he told the gringo grudgingly.

Todd raced back down the gangway and pushed his way through the crowded deck until he found the lady who was kindly guarding his rucksack. He rummaged around in the pockets until he found the mobile charger and asked a crewman to show him to the engine room.

The mechanic was as drunk as the captain and the heat in the engine room was suffocating but the man was kindly enough and he quickly pulled out some wires to power the charger. Cables sparked as the dodgy connection was made.

Todd reckoned he had never seen such a botched wiring job in his life. But miraculously the LED lights on his charger did indeed flicker into life.

'Thank you,' he told the mechanic. Todd slotted the mobile into the charging unit and watched as the little screen registered the charge. Fifteen or twenty minutes should do it, he thought, and he went back up to the deck to wait.

44

Isabella was frantically bailing out the river water from the bottom of the canoe.

No matter how fast she scooped up water there was always more flooding in.

The canoe was being dragged down the river at extraordinary speed; the trees of the riverbank were rushing past in a blur. She couldn't have held on to one even if she'd had the strength to grab it.

She could hear the sinister rumble of the rapids ahead— the low bass percussions of huge rocks being ground endlessly together on the river bed.

Then—very suddenly—the river surface changed. The spiky little wavelets, the chaos of colliding peaks of water, they all smoothed out into a mirror surface which looked as if it had been ironed flat. Isabella stared at the glassy plateau of water, transfixed with fear as she recognized this sign for what it was: the calm before the storm.

Next moment she was in the maelstrom.

It came too fast to think. The waves were too brutal and they came up with breakneck speed. The churning river was beating itself to oblivion on rock after rock and the canoe was getting pounded from all sides.

Isabella began to pray, muttering the words to the Lord's Prayer in her own language as she fought to keep the canoe upright:

'Pai Nosso, que estais nos ceus, santificado seja o teu nome . . . '
Vicious rocks. Dead ahead. Isabella grabbed the paddle, thrust it into the river and pulled with all her strength.

45

Gwen stared into the black void of the jungle for a while but saw no movement. Probably she had imagined the man's cough, she decided, and returned to the satellite call with her sister.

'What happened?' Ella asked her.

'Nothing, I'm just a bit jittery that's all. I thought I heard someone hanging around outside the mission. Anyway what's this about the Virgin Mary? I never thought of you as superstitious.'

'It's not about superstition,' Ella replied. 'I just got the weirdest feeling from that statue. Like why was it me that had to try and stop it falling? And why were there these two sharp pins on it that hurt my hands? And now they won't stop bleeding.'

'Stirrings of religion, sis?' Gwen asked, not without irony.

'I don't know, Gwen. I'm a bit freaked out by it to be honest. I just had to check you're still OK.'

'That was sweet of you, but really, I'm fine.'

Ella and her sister continued to talk for some minutes. Then she wrapped it up: 'I have to go now, Gwen. I have to take this ship into harbour. I'll talk to you soon, OK?'

They terminated the call. Gwen sighed. Sleep would be elusive now. She crossed to the window and pulled the curtain aside to stare out into the jungle. And that was when she saw a glint of moonlight on metal. Then the glow of a cigarette.

A raid. The rebel troops were gathering in the forest.

Gwen ran through the dark corridor of the mission, hurrying to wake the children.

46

Shaun's truckful of fireworks had finally reached its destination.

'We're driving on to the Harbour Bridge now,' Shaun told the radio interviewer. 'We're on a tight deadline so I have to go.'

'All right, Shaun, and good luck for tonight. The whole city will be rooting for you so make it a good one, will you?'

'You bet.' And with that the interview was terminated.

Shaun could see the cordoned off area right in the middle where the massive steel gantry was lying, waiting for the fireworks to be fitted.

Two traffic cops were signalling where to park. Shaun could see that the rest of his team had already arrived and were waiting for the goods to turn up.

Shaun jumped out of the truck and checked his watch.

'We're well over the schedule,' he told his team. 'Now let's get rigging.'

The team started to unload the fireworks from the back of the truck.

As the first dozen boxes were taken out and placed reverently on the ground, Shaun scrutinized them closely one final time for damage from the flying glass. He wanted to check every single one.

But then he was called away by the engineer in charge of the system which would winch the huge gantry into position and he told himself that everything would be all right.

As he walked away he saw a massive cruise ship approaching the harbour.

47

SYDNEY HARBOUR, QUAY NUMBER 15

The *Cayman Glory* passed beneath the Harbour Bridge at a speed of five knots and with seven metres of clearance. Almost every single one of the two thousand passengers was up on deck to savour the moment, cameras snapping busily as the mighty ship slipped by what seemed to be a whisker beneath the huge iron structure.

Ella had instructed the helmsman on the precise line to take and all had gone well. Then it was a short cruise across the harbour to quay number fifteen, one of the biggest of the cruise ship berths.

Up on the bridge it was now time for stage two of the docking procedure; again supervised by Ella with Captain Olberg standing next to her as an observer.

'All engines to neutral,' Ella instructed.

The order was confirmed from the engine room.

'Activate starboard bow thrusters,' she ordered the officer of the watch. Moments later, the twin propellers mounted in tunnels through the hull of the vessel were whirring into life.

'Stern thrusters. Half power.'

Olberg watched the process with a keen eye, ready to intervene if he saw anything that might jeopardize the vessel . . . or the dock itself.

But Ella Andersen knew her stuff and the crew were competent and fast.

The *Cayman Glory* slipped neatly sideways into the quay,

a manoeuvre which looked easy but actually required considerable skill and timing on the part of the crew. Captain
Olberg breathed easier as he felt the vessel nudge gently
against the rubber shock absorbers of the quay.

48

CENTRAL STATION, YANGON, MYANMAR, SOUTH-EAST ASIA

Wai Yan arrived at Yangon Central Station well before dawn. Many thousands of monks were already at the rendezvous spot and the young monk was mightily impressed by what he saw.

He had been on a few demonstrations in the past. But nothing like the scale of this one.

There was a determined air to the gathering, but also a strong undercurrent of fear. Previous processions had been met with a brutal response by the military government with widespread beatings of protestors, tear gas attacks, and many hundreds of monks imprisoned.

A few foreign reporters were mingling with the crowd. Their presence could only inflame the authorities.

'Brothers!' One of the lamas now stood up with a megaphone. 'We march now. And we march in peace.'

The procession set out, thousands of pairs of sandalled feet kicking up a haze of dust.

Wai Yan took his place in the column. He walked with his head held high, proud of his role as the demonstration began for he had a personal reason to be a part of the Saffron Revolution. His father had been sent to a forced labour camp (a fate shared by almost a million other victims of the Junta) where he had been starved and beaten for years before finally dying of pneumonia.

Wai Yan was firmly resolved to do his bit, and he was

determined his stance would remain peaceful no matter what provocation awaited.

And later he would tune in to the BBC to find out who Manchester United had drawn in the Champions League final sixteen.

49

Isabella was tossed from side to side, banging her ribs painfully against the wooden sides of the canoe as the rapids tried to toss her out.

Spray was soaking her from head to toe. She hit some rocks with a heart stopping crunch. The canoe started to crack up.

Then a hole opened up in the water ahead. A roaring whirlpool like a small tornado was trying to twist itself out of the river bed. The canoe plunged in. Isabella swallowed water as a wave ripped over her head. The canoe tilted, bucking as the wave tried to rip it in two.

Isabella had water up to her calves. The canoe was sinking. Both her hands were needed on the paddle. She could no longer bail it out. Her shoulders were aching. Unfamiliar muscles were being stretched to the limit as she tried to punch a route through to calmer water.

Ahead was a further terrifying sight. A two metre high wall of churning water. It was a circulating wave. A stopper. A vicious rapid just above a huge jagged rock. She was heading right for it. The paddle was flying. If she could just . . .

The roar of the water took on a deadly intensity. The bow of the canoe swung inexorably around. Not even the most powerful outboard could have countered the phenomenal pull of that wave. The vessel was a heartbeat from being crushed to matchwood and Isabella knew that all was lost.

83

Then she saw it: a final possibility. A tiny islet was jutting out of the water. It was a scrap of land, no bigger than a ping-pong table, a rocky chunk of terra firma with a couple of scrubby bushes perilously anchored in place.

Isabella jumped for her life.

50

Ella gave her final instruction to complete the docking of the *Cayman Glory*: 'Fore and aft hawsers to be deployed, please.' The huge ropes were dropped down the ship's sides, each one as thick as a man's thigh.

A few minutes later the powerful hydraulic capstans fitted to the stern and bow were winching in the hawsers until tight. 'Ship docked and in good order,' the officer of the watch told Olberg with a satisfied smile.

Olberg nodded. 'Passengers can disembark.'

Moments later he could see the huge passenger walkways being manoeuvred into place. During the next hour and twenty minutes the two thousand punters on board would be politely ushered onto dry land and bid a fond farewell. An army of cleaners would then board the vessel and blitz the cabins at inhuman speed, scrubbing, hoovering, and decontaminating until the ship gleamed with a brassy glow and stank of carpet cleaner and Windowlene.

Then, and only then, would a brand new shipload of starry eyed holidaymakers be permitted to board.

'Thank you for your help,' he told Ella.

'My pleasure, Captain. I'll see you later today for the departure.' She was already looking forward to the second part of her job; the ship would be pulling back out of the harbour to start a new cruise just a few hours later.

Ella knew it would be a more hazardous operation, for

at that point the *Cayman Glory* would be racing against the rising tide. Then the transit beneath the Harbour Bridge would be *really* tight.

51

CARGO LOADING ZONE: SYDNEY INTERNATIONAL AIRPORT

Trinny was still in the cargo area of Sydney International Airport, waiting to collect her load of lobsters. She checked her watch frequently; her contract specified a strict time slot for her delivery and she still had other pick-ups to do in western Sydney before heading to the port.

Finally the loadmaster came over. 'OK,' he told her, 'your shipment's in bay fourteen.'

Trinny reversed into the bay and opened up the rear doors. The forklift driver drove the pallets of crustaceans right into the truck, stacking them neatly in the interior until it was packed to the brim with the precious cargo.

She slammed the door shut and snapped the catch into position. 'See you,' she told the loadmaster as she jumped into the cab.

'You bet. Don't eat all those lobsters at once.'

Trinny waited for the security barrier to rise and drove out of the cargo zone. She took the slip road and joined the M5 South-Western Motorway, speeding towards the final collections of the morning.

Then the traffic slowed. Trinny put on her hazards as the vehicles around her gradually ground to a halt. She turned on the radio and caught a news item which informed her that a motorbike rider had ridden the wrong way up the freeway some time earlier, causing a number of minor crashes which had now blocked the route.

At that point she was crawling forward in the bumper to bumper traffic. Then she saw an exit which could lead her onto a rural route she had used before, an alternative which might still get her schedule to run on time. Trinny swerved off the freeway and raced up the rural road.

52

MISSION OF THE SISTERS OF CHRIST, LIBERIA, WEST AFRICA

Gwen snatched up her satphone and tucked it into the waistband of her trousers as she ran to the dormitory. She had to get the pupils awake. Try to get them out of the back of the mission before the attack began.

Some lives might be saved if they could get out of the building without being seen, melt into the darkness of the jungle.

'Wake up, children! Quickly!' she hissed. 'And don't turn on the light.'

She woke the mission's two assistants in their room and the two local girls quickly dressed and came to help her. The orphans were awake now and staring at each other with wide, terror-struck eyes.

Some began to cry. Gwen tried to comfort them as best she could.

'Be quiet now!' she told them. 'If we are quiet everything will be all right, you will see.' Minutes later they had the children up and dressed.

Gwen opened the back door to the mission. Beyond it was thick jungle. She took a step outside, her ears tuning in rapidly to the myriad chirps and croaks of night creatures.

Gwen could see no sign of the rebels in the surrounding forest here at the rear of the building. The call from Ella had enabled them to act in the nick of time as the rebels gathered at the front of the mission. Then she remembered Tehpoe, the ten-year-old boy sleeping in the sick bay. 'Go!' Gwen told the girls. 'Take the children through the forest to the town. As quick as you can.'

'What about you?' one of them asked.

'I'll fetch Tehpoe. I'll try and follow.'

53

Todd had had a frustrating wait for his mobile to be charged by the rickety old generator but finally it was done. Now he quickly climbed back up the wooden steps towards the captain's cabin and saw to his satisfaction that the signal blip on his phone had strengthened to three. Yes! Even more chance he'd be able to have a decent conversation with Hannah.

He pressed automatic redial once more but this time all he got was a man's voice, asking him to leave a message. 'This is a message for Hannah,' he said. 'Listen, you gotta get off the streets and . . . get some help. You have to promise me, OK?'

Then, frustratingly, the line went dead again.

At that moment, he saw something extraordinary. A young dark-haired girl was stranded on a small, fragile strip of land right in the middle of some rapids. She was about thirty metres across the river from the river steamer but even at that distance it was clear to him that she was in serious trouble.

'Help me! Help me!' Her cries were barely audible above the roar of the water. This was a real life drama happening right in front of his eyes. And if he hadn't climbed the steps to the captain's cabin at exactly that moment he never would have seen it.

The girl was hanging on to a small bush for dear life.

The islet was little more than the size of a table top and it seemed the water was rising. It looked as if she could be swept away by the raging river at any moment.

If that happened she would surely die. Todd stepped into the captain's cabin. He had to do something to help that girl.

54

The two assistants nodded at their instructions. Gwen knew she could rely on them. Seconds later the group had melted away into the pitch-black forest where they would be safe from the rebels. Then she heard the smashing of rifle butts against the flimsy wooden door of the mission, the cries of the drunken mob outside. Rocks rained down on the corrugated iron roof.

The attack had begun.

Gwen ran for the sick room where Tehpoe was waking with the noise. Tehpoe had been one of the first orphans Gwen had cared for at the mission. He was an intelligent and lively child but a childhood attack of TB had left him susceptible to other illnesses; for the last few days he had been confined to bed with an attack of malaria.

'It's the rebels, isn't it? Will they shoot us?' the boy whispered, his eyes two great pools of sheer terror.

'Not if I can help it,' Gwen told him.

A brittle explosion rocked the building. Smoke billowed from Gwen's bedroom and she concluded that a hand grenade must have been thrown through her window. A flash of realization hit her: the call from Ella had not only saved the lives of the children—it had prevented her from being blown to smithereens.

'Captain Kickback is coming!' screamed a voice through the broken door. The announcement was followed by manic laughter. More glass shattered. They were coming in through the windows.

'Get onto my back,' she told the terrified child. Tehpoe did as she urged, wrapping his arms around her neck with all his strength as Gwen ran for the back door of the mission.

55
CENTRAL BUSINESS DISTRICT, SYDNEY, AUSTRALIA

Marko put the final shards of glass into a box and threw them into a nearby waste container. Together with the doctor who had had his motorbike stolen he had spent the morning helping the police to clear up the mess in the street. Now they had completed the job—all bar one detail: 'What about the blood?' Marko asked the cop. There were still a few crimson stains on the pavement.

'Yeah. Doesn't look too pretty does it?' the cop agreed. 'You got a mop in the building?'

Marko fetched a cleaning trolley from the building and sluiced the pavements with disinfectant. The three of them scrubbed the patches away with mops and brushes until the street was squeaky clean.

'Nice job,' the cop told him. 'Now don't you go beating up any more butterflies, you hear me?' Marko gave a thin smile and the police vehicle pulled away.

At that moment a woman drove up in a car with two squabbling kids in the back. 'That's my wife,' the doctor told him. Marko watched as the guy greeted his wife, ruffling his kids' hair and giving them an affectionate kiss. After a brief conversation the woman handed the guy a pen drive and some cash, cracked a u-turn, and eased back into the traffic.

'That's it,' the doc told him with a smile. 'All sorted. Drama over, life goes on. I'll see you around.'

Drama over. Marko mulled over those words as he went back to his desk in the office foyer, thinking how lucky that

95

doc was to feel that way; it was as if the guy had already moved on, found some closure, dismissed the chance involvement in the event.

Drama over? Marko *wanted* to believe it, but an uneasy feeling was telling him it might not be true.

56

Wai Yan was sitting cross-legged on the concrete floor, muttering a prayer and trying to disguise his jangled nerves. The People's Park was bristling with mean looking military vehicles. A solid wall of tanks and armoured cars was lined up right in front of him.

Rumours were flying around the crowd that the military would open fire with live rounds if the protestors dared to chant or shout slogans.

The young monk had no way of knowing if such rumours were true or not but he was horribly aware that the theory might be tested quite soon. The monks had ignored the frequent calls from megaphone-wielding military men to disperse.

It was going to be a very long day. And a very long night as well. The demonstration wasn't due to end until the next morning and he was already thirsty.

To distract himself, Wai Yan decided he would discreetly check out his radio, make sure it was possible to get the BBC World Service. He knew from experience that the Junta often jammed foreign transmissions and he really didn't want to miss the draw later that day.

Who would his beloved Manchester United be paired up with, he wondered? Barcelona? Schalke? Lyon? Olympiakos? It was something to look forward to through the long and sometimes dreary monastery days.

He pulled out the earpiece and plugged it into the little

radio which was hidden in a fold of his robe. The radio was his most precious belonging, a gift from a friendly Austrian lady who had visited the monastery and taken a shine to him.

He switched the radio on but all he could hear was hiss. Wai Yan played with the dial, desperately searching for a signal.

57

Gwen was making her way through the darkened mission, racing against time to get Tehpoe out of the back door of the mission before the rebels broke in.

Once again she heard a scream: 'We have special delivery for you from Captain Kickback!'

Captain Kickback. Gwen's stomach churned with trepidation as she heard the name. The man was notorious throughout the district as one of the most ruthless and unpredictable of the rebels. Thirty years old, the commander had a penchant for mirror shades, feather head-dresses, and the disturbing habit of wearing the severed ears of his decapitated victims on a necklace around his neck.

He was an utterly quixotic devil, prone to sudden rages, his temper dictated by the random cocktail of drugs and alcohol which he habitually consumed. He was a man on the limit, permanently on the edge of extreme action. Some of his enemies put the word about that he was mentally ill.

Gwen tried to push some bed frames against the door of the sanatorium. But the gesture was futile. The rebel troops pushed their way inside the room and soon enough the commander himself entered, strutting like a drunken peacock up and down the room.

'What is your name, boy?' The commander knelt in front of Tehpoe, his face just inches away.

'Tehpoe, Commander.' The child was shaking from head to toe with terror as he stared into the commander's eyes.

'Tehpoe, eh? Well, Tehpoe, I think you are going to be a great and mighty warrior in my army!' Kickback's men cheered drunkenly and he now turned his attention to Gwen. 'And you, lady, will be my hostage!'

58

Todd entered the little wheelhouse and tapped the captain on the shoulder. As the river man turned, he could smell cheap rum on his breath. He pointed out the tiny figure of the girl clinging to the fragile chunk of land in the middle of the rapids.

'There's a girl stuck, look, there in the middle of the rapids.'

The captain looked in the direction Todd indicated, scanning the scene with experienced eyes. Then he shrugged with a thin smile and ran a finger across his throat in an unmistakable 'she's dead' motion.

'We can't just leave her,' Todd told him, 'we have to do something.'

'Bad luck. I'm not going to risk my boat for some crazy girl.' The captain turned his attention back to the task at hand, piloting the motor launch expertly up the side of the rapids.

Todd looked back at the centre of the river. He waved at the girl, shouting to give her hope: 'Hang on there!' he cried. 'We're going to come and get you!'

'Why give her false hopes?' the captain asked with a cynical smile. 'What are you going to do, swim in there and pick her up? Or order a helicopter? I'm telling you now this boat will be smashed to matchwood if I even try it so why don't you just forget about her? She won't be the first to die in these rapids and she won't be the last.'

He turned back to his wheel, bored by the conversation.

'Listen!' Todd felt the anger rising inside him. 'That girl's going to die there. We have to save her.'

59

MISSION OF THE SISTERS OF CHRIST, LIBERIA, WEST AFRICA

Commander Kickback was milking the moment for all it was worth.

He had been looking for a western hostage for a long time and now he had this woman missionary cowering before him. 'Where are you from?' he asked Gwen.

'Australia. Now please let this child go . . . he is sick, of no use to you . . . '

'*Australia?*' The commander mocked Gwen's accent.

'Please . . . '

'Shut up!' the commander roared. 'You don't understand do you? You, dear lady, have made a big mistake. You have chosen the *wrong* god!'

His men cheered. He paused to light up a huge joint of cannabis, then blew the smoke into Gwen's face before turning to his men.

'You chose Jesus! A false prophet. A man who didn't keep his promises to anyone. But you should have chosen *me*! Because I am the real provider, the one who does keep his promises and who looks after his children the proper way!'

He took off his mirror shades for a few moments, rubbing red eyes that had not seen sleep for many days. 'You two are coming with us!' he announced. 'We need some new recruits at our camp!'

'This child is too sick to go anywhere,' Gwen repeated. The commander merely laughed and ordered her to be searched. Gwen feared the satphone would be discovered but the soldier doing the frisk was so drugged he missed it. The satphone was still tucked into the waistband of Gwen's trousers as they were marched out into the jungle night.

60

Todd and the drunken captain were still arguing. Passengers were gathering around them, gawping as the row escalated. It was turning into an ugly little scene which the captain really didn't understand at all.

Who cared about that stupid kid, he wondered? What on earth was she doing trying to canoe down those rapids anyway? A kid that crazy deserved to die.

'Please,' Todd addressed his fellow travellers, thanking his lucky stars he had learned Portuguese for the trip, 'we have to save that girl.'

But the faces remained blank, uncaring. It was clear that he would get no help from them.

'If you want to be a hero there's a small encampment in the trees over there,' the captain grunted with considerable reluctance. 'You might be able to get some help there.'

Todd looked to where the captain was pointing. He saw a trickle of smoke rising from the forest canopy. Then, shaded under low branches, he saw the outline of a canoe with an outboard engine tied up against the banks of the river.

Todd thought quickly as he looked back at the girl. He could hear her thin cries for help above the roar of the rapids. Was it his imagination? Or had the level of the river already risen even more? Certainly the tiny scrap of safe ground the girl had found was looking smaller than it had ten minutes before.

'OK,' Todd said, 'let me off here.'

'I can't give you a refund on your ticket.'

'Whatever.'

61

Shaun and his team had racked their brains long and hard on the issue of what the fireworks display would be mounted on. The possibility of rigging the fireworks directly onto the superstructure of the bridge was one option, but on considering it closely, they realized that it was just too complicated and expensive to take that route.

Instead Shaun and his designers decided that this year's Sydney firework display would be fired from a custom built steel gantry, a substantial structure some fifty metres long and roughly a metre wide.

They nicknamed it 'the needle'.

This box frame structure had been constructed in ten metre sections by a local steel fabrication company and bolted together on the floor of the bridge by Shaun's fitters some days before. The electronic firing system, and the wiring it needed, were already pre-built into the frame, enabling Shaun and his team to fix the fireworks in place in a short period of time.

Once they had finished rigging the fireworks the gantry would be hoisted into position, one hundred and twenty metres above the water, close to the top of the bridge's main arch. Two radio-controlled heavy duty winches would hold the gantry precisely in position while the display took place.

It was a brilliant plan, as Shaun didn't hesitate to tell his team several times a day.

After all, he would ask them, what could possibly go wrong?

62

The nose of the riverboat nudged the riverbank. Todd jumped off, landing in boggy ground which immediately soaked his boots.

'*Adeus, amigo!*' the captain yelled, doffing his grubby cap at Todd and steering back into the centre of the river. The drama over, the passengers went back to their meals, their rum, and their games of cards.

There wasn't a moment to lose. Todd found a small trail. He followed it into the forest for fifty metres or so where he found a dirty shack in a tiny clearing. Apart from the smouldering fire there was no sign of anyone around.

'Hello?' Todd called out the greeting but the forest swallowed up the sound with no reply coming back.

He ran back to the river and took a good look at the canoe. It appeared sound enough, even if the outboard engine at the back looked pretty well destroyed. Todd wouldn't normally have dreamed of taking this boat without the owner's permission but this was a matter of life and death.

He threw in his rucksack and climbed onto the canoe.

Todd pulled the starting cord on the twenty-five horsepower unit, ripping it back with a smooth motion as the engine turned . . . and died. He paused for a few moments then tried it again, this time getting a few revolutions as a spurt of black smoke coughed out. One more go and the engine rumbled reluctantly into life.

Todd untied the rope and kicked off the bank. Then he twisted the hand grip on the outboard, feeling the bow leap up as the canoe accelerated into the current.

Moments later he felt the stupendous power of the river as he entered the rapids.

63

Hannah ran at full tilt. She found a trail, going always down-hill. Heading deeper into the canyon, the aromatic smell of eucalyptus trees all around her. Behind her the panting sound of the cop, following as fast as he could.

He didn't sound too fit, Hannah decided. At least not as fit as she was.

She kept running.

The walls of the canyon were sandstone; ancient eroded rock the colour of terracotta. Hannah looked for an exit route as she ran but all she saw was rounded, bulging cliffs with little in the way of handholds. It began to occur to her that she might be making a bad mistake; that the canyon might finish in a dead end, and that the cop would catch her there.

Hannah could hear a distant crackle—and for a second or two she thought it was fireworks, or even the cop loosing off a couple of shots.

Then another noise rippled through the trees. A 'whoosh' as trees exploded with great heat.

Hannah turned in surprise; her heart performing a triple back flip as she saw the red wall of raging flame which was already forming an impenetrable barrier across the canyon.

Fire! Like all Sydneyites Hannah had grown up with the lethal threat of fire, had seen the endless hectares of forest ravaged by it each summer, watched the news reports of

householders trapped in their homes, of firefighters who
risked their lives in the course of their work.

'Hey!' shouted the cop. 'There's a fire! We have to find a
way out.'

64

General Pauk Taw spat on the ground as he watched the monks silently take their places in the square.

Ignorant peasants, he thought. How do they think they can change anything with no weapons, no command structure, no clear objectives? He considered them pathetic and wanted nothing more than to sweep them off the streets like dead rats.

Fifty-six-year-old Pauk Taw was one of the hardliners, part of the ruling elite which was Myanmar's military command. This was the junta that had clung to power through force of arms and repression even in the face of a democratic vote which should have seen them ousted long ago.

General Taw picked up his binoculars and began to search the crowd. He was looking for familiar faces, people who could be considered ringleaders.

Then he spotted something: one of the young monks in the crowd had an earphone plugged in. He was listening to a radio, Taw was sure. A highly provocative act. He watched the boy intently for a few moments, wondering if he was taking orders from someone outside the square. The paranoid Junta had long suspected that foreign spies were the real organizers of the demonstrations.

In any case it was a perfect excuse to make a first arrest. He clicked on his walkie-talkie to speak to his next in command.

'Prepare the snatch squad,' he told him. 'We've got a target.'

65

The rebels were marching their two hostages through the night. The pace was fast and unrelenting; Gwen and Tehpoe were already stumbling with fatigue even though the slightest pause brought them an inevitable blow.

'Halt!' The commander called the procession to a stop in a clearing. The men took the opportunity to light some torches and drink some alcohol. Marijuana cigarettes were rolled and lit.

'You!' Commander Kickback pointed at Tehpoe with a terrible stare. 'I think you need a drink, boy! You seem to be a nervous soldier, and I have no place for men who do not have *courage*. So come forward and drink this, boy, and prove you are a man worthy of my command.'

Tehpoe limped forward, trying to quell the urge to cry. Then he felt the glass neck of a vodka bottle against his lips as Commander Kickback forced him to drink. The shock of the raw alcohol surging down his throat threatened to send him tumbling to the ground.

'Have you ever killed a man?' Kickback asked Tehpoe.

Tehpoe shook his head.

'You will do, boy, all in good time,' Kickback continued. 'I see a great future for you in my team, but I need to be sure of your loyalty, boy, I need to know that you answer to me!'

'Don't listen to him, Tehpoe,' Gwen said, but she was soon silenced by a savage blow to her back by one of the commander's men.

Commander Kickback put his arm around the young boy as the men started the march once more.

'You are going to be my deputy, boy!' the commander said. 'And you will have some real blood on your hands before long.'

66

Trinny checked her watch and turned up the air conditioning as she drove up the forest road.

This detour would be longer than the freeway but with a bit of luck she could still do her final pick up and be unloading the seafood bang on time. This was good news; cruise ships run extremely tight schedules for their re-supply when they are in port. Every second counts, and there are carefully planned deadlines for each delivery—run with the same efficiency as an airline departure schedule.

Trinny could lose her regular contract if she was unlucky enough to arrive late—a disaster for a business which was only barely scraping by.

Then she saw smoke drifting across the road. At first it was just a trace but it came from the canyon and Trinny knew all too clearly what that might mean.

A forest fire was raging somewhere nearby.

Trinny kept one eye on the road as she flipped open her mobile and dialled 000 for the emergency services.

'I want to report a forest fire,' she told the operator. 'I'm on the canyon road to the west of town. Can't see any flames yet but there's plenty of smoke.'

The operator took some more details and Trinny terminated the call.

She kept driving on but the smoke was drifting out of the forest in ever greater clouds. She eased her foot off the gas, taking her speed down to walking pace, aware that an

115

oncoming vehicle could suddenly loom out of the smoke in front of her.

Trinny leaned forward, staring intently out of the windscreen, watching the verge as a reference as she crept forwards. She wasn't too worried. Not yet at least. She was still more concerned about getting the lobsters to the *Cayman Glory* on time.

67

Shaun rushed back to the truck for the final box of fireworks. He was sweating like an overheated racehorse and he hadn't had time to drink or eat a scrap of food.

His team had worked their guts out but they were still pushing it on time. Fixing the fireworks into their pre-planned positions on the gantry was proving more problematic than he had expected.

The stress was crippling. Everyone was on his back and the police officer in charge of the operation was ready to give him an ultimatum.

'We have to get this gantry off the deck,' the police chief told him bluntly. 'I can't keep this traffic lane closed indefinitely. You guys made a promise to be fast and I'm holding you to it.'

'We're almost there,' Shaun told him, 'just one more box to rig . . .'

'A few fireworks more or less won't make any difference,' the policeman snapped.

Shaun bit his tongue. To him, every single firework in that display was a vital part of the show. But losing his rag with this officer wasn't going to help matters now.

'All right,' Shaun told him, 'we'll start hauling up.'

He picked up the final box of fireworks and walked over to his rigging engineers.

'Are the winches ready to go?'

'Sure.'

'OK. So let's get this sucker moving. I'll take the last box up with me and rig it when it's in position.'

68

The two fire trucks had their engines running within seconds of the call. Sydney's state of the art emergency communication system had automatically located the nearest rural station to Trinny's alert and the two five-man crews at Glenmore were even now struggling into their protective suits.

Within two minutes of the emergency call the vehicles were pulling out of the centre. The drivers hit the sirens and the trucks began to race along the wooded roads which led up to the Glenmore heights.

Fighting bush fires was the most important part of the job for the men of the Glenmore Fire Control Centre and they knew all too well the perils of a mission such as this. During one of the recent Australian bush fire periods several lives had been lost and a total of one hundred and nine houses had been destroyed, along with more than two hundred cars and more than seven thousand cattle.

But just as many lives and homes had been saved—and that was the motivation that kept these fire crews going.

In the racks behind them were oxygen sets and full face helmets which would protect them against the searing heat of the bush fire.

As the drivers hit the forest road they could already see the sinister grey haze of wood smoke rising into the clear blue sky.

'It looks like a big one,' the fire chief commented. 'I'm going to call for heli support.'

He picked up his radio handset and made the call.

69

Hannah turned as she ran, scanning the forest behind her to try and work out how serious the fire was.

Up towards the road she could see a great plume of blue-grey smoke roiling into the clear blue sky. The wind was picking up; the canyon had a funnelling katabatic effect which channelled even the slightest air current into something stronger as it was squeezed down the narrow defile.

Eucalyptus trees are particularly prone to forest fires. On very hot days they produce a haze of oil which clings close to the leaves in a highly inflammable vapour. When it is ignited the effect is like a Molotov cocktail—a fireball of terrifying speed which consumes the entire tree in an instant.

The canyon was filled with eucalyptus trees.

70

The water cannons opened up without warning; great jets aimed directly into the heart of the crowd.

Right where Wai Yan was standing.

Wai Yan had not given the water much thought. It didn't sound that frightening to be hit by what was in effect a giant garden hose. But the reality was somewhat different: the effect was like being struck by a huge fist, a strong enough impact to send the slightly built novice monk sprawling on his back amid a bundle of his comrades.

Soaked to the skin, and winded by the impact, he tried to scramble to his feet as the jet of water swept once again across the group.

He was still holding the radio in its little plastic bag.

71

Through the spray and confusion of the rapids, Todd could see the terrified face of the young girl. She was still clinging to the fragile fragment of land in the middle of the raging river, watching wide eyed as Todd battled his way towards her in the borrowed canoe.

Her lips were moving. She seemed to be chanting, or praying perhaps.

'I'm coming!' he yelled. The girl did not react.

Now Todd understood the boatman's reluctance to pilot his vessel into this part of the rapids. They were unpredictable and fierce, with waves rising so high they towered over the tiny craft. What was worse was that he could now see that the level of the river certainly *was* rising—the girl was now submerged almost to her knees.

'Hold on!' Todd yelled once more, his cry cut off prematurely as a wave sidewalled him, drenching him to the skin.

72

Hannah saw the glint of sun through the bushes—reflected on the cop's mirror shades. The sprint had winded him and he had dropped back about fifty metres in the chase.

Hannah whipped round, jumped onto a boulder to try and see down the canyon. She could see only two things. It got narrower and it got darker. But everywhere there were trees.

The fire would be blown right down between the cliffs.

Hannah knew the game had changed.

Now it wasn't about whether or not she was going to be arrested.

It was about whether or not she was going to survive.

She began to run once again. The cop still puffing away behind her.

73

Todd's canoe hit a rock. Metal graunched against granite.

It was enough to splinter the propellor. The engine screamed as Todd gave it more revs but he was being swept into the wrong channel—away from the girl he was trying to save.

He twisted the accelerator handgrip once more, begging for a few more percentage points of power from the ageing outboard.

The engine buzzed like a hornet trapped in a glass. Grey smoke spewed from the back. The entire unit was shaking itself to pieces as Todd forced it to deliver maximum load.

The canoe beat a track through the final channel. Todd swung the tiller to the right so that the vessel nudged against the islet.

The girl was almost within arm's reach.

74

Wai Yan managed to get to his feet. Victims of the water cannons were lying all over the park, demonstrators who had been smashed by the power of the water into trees or concrete benches.

Now the sinister looking tracked vehicles bearing the cannons were advancing towards the protestors with no regard for life or limb.

There was a mass panic to get away, a chaotic stampede in which Wai Yan found himself locked in the melee.

He knew if he fell again he would be trampled underfoot.

He heard gunfire. Warning shots. Sensed the rip of bullets passing through the air above the crowd.

Wai Yan sprinted for his life.

75

Trinny looked in her rear-view mirrors, seeing to her dismay that the smoke had already obscured the road behind her. She had to keep moving forward, try to get out of the area as fast as she could.

But scudding grey clouds were now obscuring the road ahead. With visibility down to almost zero, Trinny edged the truck forward, having to guess where the road was. It was no easy task and she soon realized by the bumpy terrain that she was steering off the tarmac and onto the verge.

Then came a huge *crunch*, and an upwards lurch as she ran over something large and metallic which was lying on the side of the road. With the smoke swirling ever thicker around her she had no choice but to try and keep moving but the scraping sound of metal was horrendous.

Something was stuck beneath the truck and she was now dragging it forward as she tried to escape the fire.

Trinny kept driving. It was all she could do.

76

Hannah reached the bottom of the canyon and realized that her worst fears had come true. It *was* a dead end, a U-shaped warp of rocks moulded by time into a wall of smooth sandstone cliffs which looked unclimbable.

Hannah felt tears prick at her eyes. The smoke from the fire was now billowing directly down the canyon and visibility was decreasing quickly. The flames were getting closer with every passing moment, jumping from tree to tree as the forest became an inferno.

The cop was crashing around in the undergrowth somewhere out of sight.

Hannah ran her hands over the rock but it was uniformly smooth with no welcoming handhold to grab on to. Then, on the other side of the canyon, she saw a narrow crack running in a dark split up the cliff face. She ran across, jumped up to grab it, jamming her hands into the crack and pulling up with all her strength to gain some height.

77

Wai Yan hurdled several rose beds, crashed through a hedge as the cries of his fellow monks rang in his ears, each sharp *crackle* of the guns provoking a new wave of panic.

Tanks were grinding across the roadways to the square. Wai Yan could see that the exits were being blocked.

The warning shots had finished. Now the troops were firing directly at the backs of the running monks. They were baton rounds—non-lethal rubber bullets—but they could still put a man in hospital for a week.

Wai Yan looked back as he ran; saw one of the soldiers pointing directly at him. The man barked an order to one of the tanks and it swivelled towards the young monk.

Now Wai Yan got it. For some reason it was *him* that was being targeted, *him* they were after. Then he saw a building across the street. A few fellow demonstrators had already rushed inside.

Wai Yan followed them.

78

Todd could see that the girl was bleeding from a cut to her head, that her knees were also bruised and bloodied.

'Jump!' Todd shouted above the roar of water.

The girl shook her head.

'Now!' But she stayed stock still.

Todd was close enough that he could see the girl was trembling, her hands locked in a white knuckle embrace around the scrappy shrub which was her anchor. She seemed paralysed, unwilling to place herself once more in the tumbling terror of the river.

Todd stepped half off the canoe, grabbed the girl by the arm and lifted her on board. She slumped into the bottom of the canoe as he pushed away into the current.

And that was when the engine died.

79

Hannah was halfway up the cliff.

She jumped up. Two fingers of her right hand jammed into the crack. She pulled up with a supreme effort and got her left hand onto the lip. Her sneaker found a little cluster of crystals to rest on as she straightened up her leg.

Seconds later she was on the top. She slumped to the ground, exhausted by the climb and racked by a series of deep coughs as her lungs tried to expel the ever thicker smoke.

She stood. She knew she had to keep moving or the fire would surely catch her in the end. But what about the cop? She knew he was as good as dead if she left him now.

Hannah had her wild side but she couldn't knowingly let someone die when there was a chance he could be saved.

She had to get him out of the canyon.

'Over here!' she called down. 'There's a way up the cliff here.'

80

General Pauk Taw watched intently as the young monk dived into the doorway. Seconds later the huge door slammed shut and he could hear the high pitched rasp of metal bolts as the lock was drawn.

'Wait here!' he ordered his driver.

On his orders, half a dozen soldiers were soon pushing against the door but there were thirty or forty demonstrators inside and they were holding them off.

General Pauk Taw climbed back into his mobile command post and rapped on the roof of the armoured vehicle. The vehicle inched forward through the troops until the cow bars on the front were nudging against the door.

'Smash down the door!' he ordered the driver. 'Forward!'

81

From the moment the engine died the canoe was doomed.

The girl was continuing to mutter her prayer, her face now white with fear.

Todd wished she would keep quiet. Her praying sounded too much like a final plea and Todd was pretty sure that no one was listening.

Finally the boat slid right over the top of a particularly vicious rock. The vessel fractured into several pieces, the rear end with the heavy engine attached sinking first and taking the rucksack with it.

Todd felt the grip of the river, the chill factor as the surprisingly cold water drew heat away from his body. The girl was drowning, her arms flailing as she tried to keep her head above water. Todd swam a few strokes and grabbed her, pulling her head up.

'Swim! You have to swim!'

The girl snatched at his shoulders, her panic giving her surprising strength. Todd was pushed under for a few seconds, then bobbed up as he managed to turn the girl's body away from him.

82

Trinny managed to get clear of the smoked-out area. She climbed out of the truck and inspected the underside, seeing to her amazement that there was a charred wreck of a burned out *motorbike* jammed underneath it.

She inspected the damage, seeing immediately that the front tyre was completely shredded. At that moment a fire tender came racing around the corner and Trinny figured she had never seen a sweeter sight in her life.

The fire crew were as mystified as Trinny was about how a riderless motorbike came to be jammed under her truck but they quickly got to work. In less than a minute they had a hi-lift jack in place and had raised the vehicle enough for two of the burly firefighters to pull out the motorbike.

'Where's your spare tyre?' the firechief asked. 'We have to get you on the move.'

83

Hannah watched as the cop attempted—and failed—to scramble up the cliff on the same route. 'It's hopeless. I can't do it,' the cop told her, his voice cracking with fear as the flames raged ever closer.

Hannah took stock of her immediate surroundings, realizing for the first time that there was a forest clearing right next to her, a place where kids had built a small den out of branches.

Then, on the other side of the clearing she saw a length of rope—a kids' swing—hanging loose from a tree.

Hannah ran across the clearing. She pulled hard on the rope but whatever kid had tied it to that high branch had done a good job and she couldn't shift it.

Now the smoke was rolling up over the canyon lip, and Hannah found herself gagging with it as her lungs began to fill. She pulled the hood of her jacket over her face to give some protection from the heat.

'Aigh!' She recoiled as a sharp pain cut through her fingers.

84

Wai Yan managed to jump backwards as the door was breached. The snout of an army vehicle punched through the splintered timber, the horn blaring aggressively.

The demonstrators bolted through the dust, ducking for cover in the dark corners of the municipal storehouse.

'That's him!' came a cry.

Wai Yan began to sprint down the aisles of the depot building, the racks on either side of him filled with gardening equipment, traffic signs, and other city stuff. The armoured car was tracking him, squeezing down the aisle as it hunted him down.

The troops were close. A rubber bullet whistled past Wai Yan's shoulder. It was so near he could feel the wind rush of the passing projectile.

Wai Yan turned and put up his hands.

'OK,' he said. 'Don't fire. Don't shoot!'

85

Todd was swallowing water. Every snatched breath was threatening to be his last. But he kept swimming, holding the girl by her hair in a desperate attempt to keep her head above water.

Then he had a sudden flash of memory. A survival programme he'd once seen on television. Advice on how to survive fast moving water. What had they said: keep your feet pointing downstream? That was it! Protect the head at all costs. Todd manoeuvred his body into the correct position, drawing the girl alongside him and supporting her head with his right arm.

The current was easing off, losing power as the river entered the bend. Todd reckoned he should be striking out for the far side—the side which meant Porto Velho and safety—but he knew instinctively that he could never make it across the three hundred metre wide river with the girl in his arms.

So he did the only thing he could: let the current sweep both of them into the bank where he could grab hold of some branches and pull them both to the shore.

86

The fire crew tightened up the last of the wheelnuts on Trinny's truck. They bade her a quick farewell and drove off towards the fire, which was now flaring up viciously towards the canyon.

Trinny checked her watch. She could still make it to the port but she would have to think clearly and act fast. There was no time for those extra pick ups now.

Before she got moving, Trinny got down on her back and squirmed under the truck. She was checking to see if the motorbike had caused any other damage. She figured that it might have punctured the fuel tank or punched a hole in the exhaust. But her quick visual check revealed no dripping fluid, or other sign of damage.

If she'd looked a bit harder she would have seen the handbrake cable—completely severed. But she didn't spot it.

Trinny climbed back into the truck and raced off down the road, heading for the city and her rendezvous with the cruise ship.

87

Hannah sucked on her bleeding fingers for a few moments then she stood—and shook the hood to try and loosen whatever was in there.

She realized there was something stuck in the hood. For a heartbeat or two Hannah thought it was a spider or even a snake, so intense was the pain she experienced.

A seven centimetre long shard of razor sharp glass fell out onto the forest floor.

Hannah stared at it, bewildered for a moment, then realized where it had come from. The flying glass impacting into the street back in downtown Sydney. This piece had got lodged in the hood of her jacket.

She grabbed the shard of glass, reached up as high as she could and began to cut through the strands of the rope.

88

Todd and the girl made it to the shore, or at least to a dark pool where they could stand without being swept away. Dense trees were hanging over the spot—making it tightly enclosed, giving it the feeling of a cave.

In those moments the sun went down and night embraced the scene.

No starlight could penetrate that canopy but luckily Todd remembered that he had a waterproof headtorch in his jacket pocket.

It was still there.

Todd turned on the precious beam of light. And that was when he realized they had a further problem.

Instead of a good firm bank, the side of the river was almost vertical. It was a wall of mud. A slippery face of glutinous slime some five metres high. It looked like an impossible climb.

Their nightmare was by no means over.

89

THE PEOPLE'S PARK, YANGON, MYANMAR, SOUTH-EAST ASIA

General Pauk Taw strutted up to the terrified young monk. He snatched the little radio from his hands and ripped the plastic bag away to examine it.

The military man could see immediately that this was not the walkie-talkie he had expected. It was, however, a short-wave radio which could receive transmissions from foreign lands, and that in its own right could be used against the boy.

'Owning such a radio is illegal,' he said with some satisfaction. 'What are you doing with it?'

'I wanted to listen to the football . . . the Champions League draw,' Wai Yan whispered through trembling lips.

'*Football?*' the general replied, his face incredulous. 'Don't take me for an *idiot*. This is a device to communicate with foreign spies.'

The general put the radio in his pocket. 'Bring him out to the square,' he said. 'I want to talk to the crowd.'

90

Hannah cut the final strands. The section of rope was free. She ran to the edge of the cliff. She lowered the rope down the face. The smoke was now so thick she could hardly see the cop just a couple of metres below her position.

'I got it!' the cop yelled as he grabbed the rope. Hannah felt the man's weight. She had to brace with her feet, stressing the sinews in her arms so they felt they would burst as she eased him up the cliff face.

He reached the lip of the cliff. Pulled himself up and collapsed next to Hannah.

'Thank God,' he managed to gasp. 'Now we gotta get out of here.'

A moment later they were running, pounding down the forest trail towards the road where they could even now hear sirens and the sound of a helicopter.

91

Todd could see that the girl was getting very cold. He was also tiring fast and beginning to shiver with the chill effect of the water.

He saw two exposed roots jutting out of the bank, grabbed hold of them and pulled with all his strength, only to find that they both broke under the pressure. He slid back down to the bottom of the bank, covered in filthy slime and breathing hard with the effort.

'Try again!' the girl urged him. 'We can't stay here.'

Todd clambered up the bank again, getting a little bit higher but finding no easy way out; right at the top of the formidable mud wall was a dense mass of exceptionally thick vegetation—a chaos of thorns and entangled vines which looked totally impenetrable.

Pushing through it would tear him to shreds.

'Maybe you can swim across to the town?' the girl proposed.

Todd thought about it then shook his head. He had no more strength to battle that savage current.

92

Hannah and the cop burst out of the forest and reached the safety of a tarmac road. They breathed a sigh of intense relief as they saw what was waiting for them there.

Three huge fire trucks were already in attendance and a rescue helicopter was landing close by. The firemen greeted the traffic cop with surprise when they saw him standing there with his face blackened with smoke.

'Are there any more in the canyon?' one of them asked.

Hannah and the cop shook their heads and then sat side by side on the verge, exhausted by their ordeal. For a couple of moments they watched the fire team as they raced into action.

'OK,' Hannah said. 'What happens next?'

The cop gave her a stony look.

'We're going to get some treatment and then I'm going to arrest you,' he said. 'I know I owe you one for dragging me out of that canyon but I'm still going to do you for stealing the bike, reckless driving, and a bunch of other stuff.'

At that moment a paramedic with a backpack ran over from the helicopter. He examined them both and found first degree burns to Hannah's hands and arms and the same to the cop's legs where his trousers had been burnt through.

He doused their wounds with cool water and applied cold compresses as a first aid measure. 'We'll medivac you two to the nearest clinic,' he said. 'You both need treatment.' He motioned to the helicopter pilot to start up the rotors.

Then he escorted Hannah and the cop towards the waiting chopper.

93

The rebel division of Commander Kickback arrived with their prisoners at their remote jungle camp a few hours before dawn. Gwen and Tehpoe were on their last legs, exhausted by the relentless speed of the march through the night and suffering deeply from the stress of their captivity.

Gwen took a good look around the ramshackle camp, wondering if there was anywhere else on earth which so closely resembled hell. The decomposing bodies of three government soldiers were lying dead in the middle of the scrappy clearing, another was hanging dead from the low branch of a tree, his body riddled with gunshot wounds.

A few shacks were dotted around the perimeter of the clearing and, set back into the jungle, a more substantial bungalow with an iron roof which was evidently the commander's headquarters. Vicious dogs could be heard snarling inside it.

'Welcome to the Kickback Hilton!' the commander roared as he took centre stage in the middle of the clearing. 'In the morning we will issue a demand to the people of Australia,' he continued. 'Ten million dollars for the life of a missionary! What do you think, men?'

'Not enough! More!' they replied, letting off gunfire into the night sky.

The commander laughed. 'Very well. Let us say twenty million and we'll settle for that.'

'No one will pay it,' Gwen protested.

'Oh, but they will,' the commander told her. 'If it is necessary I will send little pieces of you until they take me seriously. Now I think it is time to get some rest.'

94

Shaun and a colleague were having the ride of their lives as the winch slowly ground away, the gantry rising smoothly up to the high point of the Harbour Bridge.

Perched on the tiny platform, secured by waist harnesses to a guard rail, they were treated to the most spectacular view imaginable; the opera house, the myriad ferries buzzing about the bay, the city itself, resplendent and gleaming with brilliant sunlight.

It was a slow journey but the winches were performing well, hauling the huge gantry and its load of fireworks inch by inch up to the final position on the top of the central arch. The 'gunpowder geek' was now way above the deck of the bridge and he felt a tinge of nausea as vertigo hit; he was not so used to working on high platforms and he couldn't help noticing that the steel cables gave out an occasional alarming creak as they flexed under the weight.

Nevertheless he welled up with pride as the contraption rose; the plan was working a treat and virtually all of the fireworks were in their pre-planned positions. Only that one box remained to be rigged up and Shaun reckoned that they would be abseiling down before long.

Shaun eased his finger off the remote control device for the winch as the gantry reached its destination. There was a gentle shudder as the steel frame came to a halt. Shaun clicked on his walkie-talkie: 'Gantry in position.'

'Roger that. Nice work, mate.'

He opened up the final box. There they were: the Multi Break Shells, Horsetails, Spiders, Chrysanthemums, Fish, Peonies and Rings. Their colour effects were pre-determined: strontium for red, sodium for yellow, barium for green, and copper halides for the blues.

Shaun picked one of the fireworks out and got to work.

95

Fifteen minutes later the helicopter flared into a hover and touched down at the Glenmore Clinic helipad. Hannah and the cop had sat in awkward silence for most of the flight.

Hannah's mood had soured; this really was her day from hell. Fleabilly had been killed in that freak accident, she had been injured in the fire and now she was firmly back in the hands of the authorities.

Accordingly, when the paramedic asked them curiously, 'What were you two *doing* down in that canyon?' Hannah's reply was caustic:

'Having a picnic,' she snapped. The man didn't ask any more questions.

Now the air ambulance powered down as a small team of medics approached with stretchers. 'I'm OK to walk,' Hannah told them. 'But a couple of pain killers wouldn't be a bad idea.' The burns to her arms were now agonizingly painful.

The two patients were escorted through to a treatment room and the cop patiently responded as his personal details and blood group were entered into a PDA.

As for Hannah, there was only one thing on her mind at this moment:

Getting the heck out of that hospital.

Even as the orderlies peeled back her temporary dressings to inspect the damage, her eyes were flicking to the window and calculating her chances of a getaway on foot.

'Hope you're not thinking about trying to escape?' the cop said sternly. He instructed one of the nurses to shut down the window. 'Lock it,' he told her. 'I'm not losing her a second time.'

96

Trinny checked her watch as she raced up the access ramp which would take her into the port area. She was now embarrassingly late for her scheduled 'slot' with the *Cayman Glory* and she knew that there would be hell to pay with the ship's quartermaster.

She reached the loading area where the cranes and forklift vehicles were busy unloading other delivery trucks.

A marshall in a high-viz jacket waved her onto one of the delivery ramps. Trinny parked up and pulled on the handbrake. She jumped out of the cab and walked quickly to the little glass booth where the security guard was waiting to check her papers.

'What's your load schedule, sweetheart?' he asked.

Trinny was checking the papers to give him the correct reference number when she saw the man's eyes widen in alarm. 'Hey!' he shouted. Trinny spun round. Too late.

The handbrake had failed. Trinny's earlier accident with the motorbike had severed the cable which it depended on. The truck was moving. Slipping backwards down the ramp. Towards the ship.

Trinny sprinted to the cab but she wasn't fast enough to catch it. The truck had picked up too much momentum and was moving backwards, heading straight for the dockside and the gleaming white hull of the *Cayman Glory*. The refrigerated truck slipped backwards over the edge of the dock and smashed into the hull of the cruise ship.

It was wedged between the ship and the dock wall.

Trinny clamped a hand to her mouth in horror as the dock workers came running to the scene.

97

Todd explored the area a bit more, realizing with a sinking sensation that they had no realistic options. They couldn't swim out without taking an incredible risk—the river was way too forceful for that—but they couldn't make it onto dry land either.

'We have to get out of the water,' he told her. 'Maybe we can sit on this branch.'

Todd lifted up the girl and placed her on the only branch which was low enough to reach. Then he clambered up alongside her. It was a difficult manoeuvre to haul himself out of the pool and he was shocked by how weak his arms felt.

There was just enough space on it to take the two of them—but Todd didn't like the ominous creaking noises the branch made as it took their weight.

There was only one thing for it, he realized: they would have to stay put for the night.

'We'll be OK,' he told the shivering girl. 'Someone will rescue us in the morning, you'll see.'

'Maybe by then it will be too late,' the girl sobbed.

'What do you mean?'

'I'm trying to fetch a doctor,' the girl said quietly. 'I have to get one for my mother. She's supposed to be having a baby but there are problems . . . '

'That's why you tried the rapids? To get help for your mother?'

The girl nodded miserably and Todd was overcome with admiration for her bravado. To try and paddle that killer section of river had been an act of raw courage. As the final glimmer of daylight died, Todd placed his arm around the girl's shoulders to try and keep her warm.

98

Captain Olberg was taking a shower in his stateroom on board the *Cayman Glory* when a loud knock at his cabin door caught his attention. 'Accident on the dock,' his first officer told him. 'We've got a truck wedged against the hull.'

Olberg dried himself off in record time and joined his officer on the bridge from where they could look directly down onto the scene below.

From his location on the bridge deck he could see immediately the severity of the situation. The delivery truck had wedged itself tightly into the gap between the dock wall and the steel hull. Even if the back of the vehicle hadn't punched a hole in the hull, it might yet damage the cruise ship further as it was extricated from the position.

'Bloody idiot driver,' Olberg cursed to his first officer. 'Let's go down and take a look.'

Five minutes later Olberg and two of his senior officers were standing on the dock. They discussed the situation with the ship's engineer as they assessed the best way to get the truck out. 'We need to get a rigger down there. Weld some steel cables onto the truck's chassis,' Olberg instructed. 'Then we need a heavy-lift crane to pull it out.'

Olberg's officers jumped to it and the captain returned to his cabin and instructed his PA to track down the ship's owner who was at that moment on holiday somewhere in Asia.

Small incidents were an inevitable part of cruising life. An elderly passenger dying on board. A few cases of food poisoning. These were things which the captain didn't need to trouble the owner about. But this was different: the ship had actually been damaged and Olberg knew he would have to inform the *Cayman Glory*'s owner about the accident.

A short time later, less than a kilometre from the People's Park where Wai Yan had recently been arrested, a telephone call buzzed in an office of the Cosmos Hotel. The manager listened for a few moments and scribbled a note to give to a bellboy who left immediately in search of a guest.

The guest was John Hicks, the owner of the *Cayman Glory*, a self-made businessman who had built his Australian shipping company up the hard way through his own blood, sweat, and tears. Now Hicks and his wife were on holiday in Myanmar, waiting in the lobby of the hotel for a car to take them on a city tour.

'Mr Hicks, sir, there's a fax coming through for you.'

Hicks frowned at the news. Holiday time was precious and he had an unspoken understanding with his wife that he would not get sidetracked by business affairs while they were travelling together.

But the thought of a fax coming through was distracting—and not a little troubling. Hicks had left firm instructions with his office that he was only to be contacted in the event of a problem with his pride and joy—the *Cayman Glory*.

'Forget it, John,' his wife Fran snapped. 'It's only a stupid fax.'

But Hicks couldn't let it go. He knew that the *Cayman Glory* was docking in Sydney that very morning and he was concerned there might be a problem with the turn around. A delay in the schedule could mean huge losses and Hicks's cruise business was already operating on wafer slim margins as a result of the global downturn.

'I'll be back in a moment,' he told them.

Commander Kickback's soldiers grabbed hold of Gwen and began to drag her across the parade ground.

'Hold my hand, Tehpoe! We have to stay together!'

The young orphan clutched Gwen's hand with all his might but they were soon torn apart and taken to different parts of the camp.

Gwen was thrown into a makeshift cell containing just a foul smelling mattress and a bucket. Bats erupted from the roof as she was pushed inside and a second later she was confronted by Commander Kickback's leering face at the barred window.

'Do you still think that God exists?' he hissed.

He stumbled off into the night, cackling hysterically as Gwen collapsed against the wall.

Then she felt it, hard against her back. The satellite phone. It was still tucked into the waistband of her trousers.

She pulled out the unit and offered a brief but heartfelt prayer of thanks to God. A lifeline.

Then she paused; what if it made a noise when it was activated? Did the unit bleep a welcome when it was turned on? If a guard heard it then all hope would be lost.

She simply couldn't remember.

A burst of gunfire ripped through the night air. One of Kickback's drugged-up soldiers shooting at goodness only knew what. Gwen used the noise as cover, pressed the 'on' button on the phone and held her breath.

101

As he walked back into the square, General Pauk Taw was amazed to find that almost all of the monks had already returned to their places.

The general had to concede there was a curious power to these demonstrations. The international press had taken a keen interest in them, and, for the first time, Pauk Taw had detected the beginning of a split at the heart of the military command. A new generation of younger, more moderate commanders was coming up through the ranks.

Dangerous fools.

The general climbed up on the nearest tank. He snatched a megaphone from one of his officers and began a furious diatribe against the protestors.

'Criminal elements! You are leeches!' he screamed at the monks. 'Why don't you go and work in the fields where you can be useful? But no! All you want is books, and ideology, and words! Don't you understand that you have been tricked? Manipulated by agencies of the west?'

The general had Wai Yan brought up next to him. The boy was shaking so much with terror he could hardly stand upright.

'And now we have proof!' the general yelled as he held Wai Yan's little radio aloft. 'This terrorist has been caught communicating with foreign spies. Taking orders from his

161

paymasters in the CIA, at MI5! He will be vigorously inter-
rogated and the truth will be told.'

Wai Yan was bundled violently off the tank and dragged
away to one of the armoured cars. He was pushed inside
and the door was slammed shut.

Still the monks did nothing, merely bowed their heads in
silent prayer.

102

Ship's carpenter Bruce Tiler was on deck five at that moment. The carpenter had spent the best part of three hours disassembling the huge nativity scene and was now hauling a trolley towards the offloading bay with the heavy resin figurines on it.

The weird accident with the Virgin Mary figurine had been upsetting to say the least. The woman—the pilot—had put a brave face on it but those two wounds on her palms had looked bad. Bruce blamed himself for it—and try as he might, he couldn't quite shake off the feeling of guilt.

Bruce made his way to the offloading bay and was just about to commence the task of putting the figurines onto a pallet to be lifted off the ship when the sweating figure of Doug the supervisor appeared in the doorway.

'Change of plan, buddy. We need you down on the dock,' the supervisor told him. 'Some truck hit the ship. There's going to be some painting repairs so take your roller down.'

'What about Jesus and his mates?'

Bruce gestured to the collection of religious figurines which were stacked in the corner of the bay.

The loadmaster checked his watch.

'We won't have time to offload them,' he said. 'Put them in the storeroom and we'll get rid of them next time we're in port.'

Bruce nodded.

He sighed, then turned the trolley round and started to pull the figurines back towards the cargo lift.

103
RIO JARI, AMAZON BASIN, BRAZIL

Todd knew that he had to keep the girl awake. Their situation on that feeble branch was precarious to say the least and he feared she would tumble into the river and be swept away if she fell asleep. Only by keeping her morale up would she make it through the night. She had been sobbing non-stop since their ordeal began.

'What's your name?' Todd asked her.

'Isabella.'

'I'm Todd. Let me see that cut.'

Todd examined the cut on the side of the girl's face with his torch, saw that it was deep enough to require some stitches. Those would have to wait until they were safe.

'Tell me about your family,' Todd asked her kindly.

For a while they swapped stories, Isabella telling Todd about the hunting expeditions she had been on with her father, Todd telling her about some of the adventures he had had on his journey through South America.

'The problem is, I can't stop thinking about my mother,' the girl told him. 'She's in so much pain.'

'We're going to get help for her, just as soon as we can,' he told her. 'Do you think you'll be strong enough to swim across the river when it is light?'

The girl hung her head and did not reply and Todd reassured her that a boat would come even if they could not swim. Later Todd pulled his mobile out of his pocket and shone his torch on the screen. He knew it was a hopeless thought but he had to try it anyway. Of course it was flooded, totally destroyed, and he threw it away in disgust.

He thought about his sister Hannah, wondering how she was and hoping she was OK.

104

Captain Olberg supervised as a rigger was sent down on a line. The man welded two steel cables to the front axle of the truck and the stay lines of the vessel were loosened off as the truck was slowly winched up.

'Slow and steady!' the captain commanded the driver. He flinched as he heard the nerve-jangling sound of metal scraping against metal as the back of the truck cut a scar into the shiny white paintwork of the immaculate ship. Passengers were gawping at the scene as they boarded the vessel.

With the truck winched up, Olberg and his men could see the extent of the damage. There was a dented area about two metres long where the rear axle of the truck had fallen back against the ship. Then there was plenty of scraping and ugly scratches but they were largely cosmetic. The hull had not been breached. That was the important thing. 'Looks like we might have got away with it,' Olberg said.

But he still wanted to be sure. 'I want a structural engineer down here with an ultrasound unit,' Olberg told his first officer. 'Check the hull is sound.'

'Right away, sir.'

'Get the rest of the loads on board,' Olberg ordered his quartermaster. 'We're really pushing it on time now.'

Captain Olberg took a look at his watch. The incident with the truck must have cost them a good hour of the loading schedule. That wouldn't have been so serious if they'd been staying the night in port, but this was a turn around day without an overnight stop and they had to be sailing on schedule or they'd miss the low tide which would allow them to get out beneath the Harbour Bridge.

It was going to be really, really tight.

105

For the last forty minutes, security guard Marko had had his mother on the phone. The TV news reports had been seen by members of his family and now he was doing as good a job as he could of trying to calm her down.

'Are you wearing your charm?' his mother asked him urgently. Marko sighed. His mother was of Greek descent and was forever giving him lucky amulets to ward off the evil eye.

'Of course I am,' he lied. Marko checked his watch. It was almost time to finish his shift. 'I'm finishing work now,' he told his mother, 'don't you worry about a thing.'

The guard taking over the next shift arrived as Marko terminated the call. Marko brought the guy up to date on what had happened and took him up to the floor to show him where the butterfly incident occurred.

'Teach you for trying to kill one of God's creatures,' the guy said. Marko wasn't laughing at that one.

As he changed out of his uniform Marko tried to be positive; maybe he was better off thinking about how lucky he had been with that falling pane of glass. There was no need to feel so bad, he figured. So far as he could see, no terrible harm had been done. A dog had been killed, a motorbike had been stolen, it was true. A couple of cars had bent fenders. A few people with cuts. But compared to how it could have been? Marko knew he had got away lightly.

Marko left the building and walked towards Central Station. He knew that Denise was waiting for him at home but his mind was still mulling over the freak events connected with that butterfly. He suddenly felt strangely unsettled, curiously on edge.

He decided to go for a coffee.

106

In the foyer of the Cosmos Hotel, John Hicks's wife Fran was beginning to get stressed. Her husband had disappeared into the manager's office to read his precious fax and their chauffeur-driven car had failed to turn up. Rumours were going around amongst the hotel guests that there was a big anti-government demonstration taking place in the centre of the city. Fran hoped their tour wouldn't be delayed because of trouble.

Finally Hicks was back. 'Sorry, love. Bad news from Sydney, seems some damn idiot let their van fall into the side of the *Cayman Glory*.'

'Oh.' Fran's tone modified a little to a slightly warmer shade; she knew how important the cruise ship was to her husband's remaining business.

'They're pulling it clear with a crane. Just have to hope they make it out of the harbour on the low tide or I'll be down a packet.'

Fran understood enough about the business to know what her husband was saying. The berth fee for an extra night at Sydney harbour for a cruise ship like the *Cayman Glory* would be little short of 20,000 dollars, let alone the knock-on effect of having to cancel an overnight for the vessel at Fiji or Auckland and the ever present threat of being sued by irate passengers.

At that moment their chauffeur arrived. 'Sorry to be late,' the driver told them politely, 'but we should leave straight away.'

'Give me one more minute,' Hicks said. 'I really must reply to this fax.'

'Oh, for goodness' sake, John!' Fran raised her eyes to the heavens as her husband retreated back to the office.

DECK THREE: THE *CAYMAN GLORY*, SYDNEY HARBOUR

The officer of the watch gave his report to Captain Olberg. 'They've done an ultrasound check on the welds. The hull is perfectly sound, sir,' he told him.

'Very good.' Olberg looked down at the shore level; he could see the painting crew had already managed to cover up most of the scratching with marine grade white paint.

Then the officer continued, 'Just the question of the lobsters, sir.'

'The lobsters?'

'That's what's in the van.'

Olberg swore beneath his breath.

'All right. I'll give you ten minutes. But if they're not on board by then we're sailing without them and the guests will just have to do without.'

The officer of the watch rushed off to supervise the process. Olberg followed him, watching intently from the cargo loading deck. Down on the dock he could see the many boxes of the live crustaceans being loaded from the damaged van into a cargo net.

Olberg continued on his tour of inspection, arriving at the embarkation point where the fresh batch of passengers were now boarding. There was a photographer snapping them as they came on board and Olberg decided to greet a few of the new arrivals with a handshake and a smile.

A couple came down the gangplank towards him. An

attractive woman in her thirties and a man of a similar age in a wheelchair.

'Welcome on board,' the captain greeted them warmly.

'This way for a souvenir shot,' said the photographer.

'We don't want a photo,' the disabled man said firmly.

The couple moved away briskly to search for their cabin.

108

Gwen watched the satphone as it flickered into life. The red glow of the screen seemed as bright as a thousand watt floodlight in the pitch black of her little cell and she shielded it beneath her jacket. Salty drips of sweat streamed from her brow as she stared feverishly out into the compound.

A guard could look in through the bars of the cell at any moment.

In the top left-hand of the screen was a tiny graphic of an antenna; next to it were the bar indicators which told the user how many satellites had been captured. Gwen knew that her position near the equator meant there was a plethora of communication satellites within range and, sure enough, the unit was quickly hooked up to five orbiting devices.

Gwen heard urgent voices near the door. The guards were arguing about something and it occurred to her that if she could hear them then they would certainly be able to hear her. She couldn't risk a voice call.

A text. That was the solution. A text to one of the workers at the charity headquarters in Geneva. Or, failing that, she could text Ella in Sydney.

She stabbed at the unit. Where was the function which would let her do it? Increasingly desperate, she scrolled through the menu, finding sophisticated functions that she never knew existed.

But no function that would let her send a text.

She wasn't being dumb. Most satphones have no such facility. She would have to wait. Make the call later when she was absolutely certain that the guards were asleep. For the first time in her life, Gwen began to feel that God might have deserted her.

109

COSMOS HOTEL, YANGON, MYANMAR, SOUTH-EAST ASIA

John Hicks returned from sending his fax and joined his wife and the chauffeur outside the hotel.

'Look at that!' Fran told him. At the far end of the street was a startling sight: a solid column of marching monks. A new trainload had arrived at the central station and were now proceeding to join their brothers in the People's Park.

'This is a problem,' the driver said. 'We will have to wait for the procession to pass.'

'Ridiculous!' Hicks raised his eyebrows to heaven and ushered his long-suffering wife into the car.

'Darling, don't get stressed,' she warned him protectively, 'you know what the doctor said about your heart.'

Hicks snorted and buried his head in a week-old edition of the *Herald Tribune*. If it had just been down to him, Hicks might have decided to junk the tour. He reckoned he had seen enough gilded pagodas to last him a lifetime but he didn't want to disappoint his wife.

'What time do you think we'll be able to leave?' Hicks checked his watch yet again. The driver just shrugged.

A convoy of military vehicles rushed past. Hicks stepped out of the car and looked down the street. The crowd was almost upon them. He could hear chanting and the soft shuffle of feet. The military vehicles had already gone ahead, vanishing around the corner.

'Revolting monks!' he snapped to his wife. 'What the hell next?' Now the huge crowd was filing past them.

'Some of them are just children,' Fran said in astonishment.

110

The man in the wheelchair who had just refused the boarding photo on the *Cayman Glory* was called Murray West. The woman with him was Tammy Simons, his long-time lover . . .

. . . and partner in crime.

A resident of Melbourne, Murray's birth thirty-four years earlier had been a complicated and protracted affair which had left him partly paralysed with cerebral palsy. He had been a wheelchair user since the age of five. His mind, however, was sharp as a razor. Sharp enough to have made a small fortune as a successful thief specializing in cruise ship work with Tammy at his side.

No one ever suspects that someone in a wheelchair could be a criminal; a fact that Murray and Tammy had capitalized on ruthlessly in their quest to enrich themselves at others' expense.

'Welcome on board,' Olberg had told the passengers as he shook the couple by the hand. 'I hope you enjoy the voyage.'

We'll enjoy the voyage, Murray was thinking as he thanked the captain with a smile, but not for the reasons you think.

Now, Murray pressed the control stick forward with his right hand, steering his electric wheelchair towards the lift as Tammy followed on. They descended into the depths of

179

the vessel to the eighth floor and made their way to their modest two-berth cabin.

'When do you want to start?' Tammy asked him after they had stowed their bags.

'No time like the present. Why don't we try the restaurant?'

Murray led the way as they headed back to the lifts. The thrill of the hunt gave him a buzz of pleasure as he gave their fellow passengers a charming smile.

111

Bruce had just finished his painting repair job on the ship's hull when his walkie-talkie buzzed into life yet again. Bruce stared at the unit with some venom. On days like this, when the jobs kept coming thick and fast, he truly wished he could throw the irritating thing into the bay.

'Get your arse back on board will you, Bruce?' snapped the supervisor with his customary charm. 'We're short handed up on the load deck.' Bruce quickly stashed his brushes and roller in a work trolley and took the crew lift up to deck three.

When he arrived at the loading zone he found the place in a state of considerable chaos. 'Grab that hoist will you?' Doug ordered him. 'There's a load of lobsters to bring up.'

It was the first time that Bruce had operated the cargo hoist system on his own but he was a practical guy and he figured it out fast enough. The net filled with the lobster boxes came up smoothly and Bruce worked out how to swing the small crane across by hand so that they could be lowered onto the deck.

The boxes were offloaded and Bruce pressed the winch button to bring the net back up. What he hadn't noticed was that the net was spinning gently as he raised it—and that a part of the net was caught on a shackle welded to the deck.

The net snagged. Bruce fumbled at the winch control but he wasn't familiar enough with the unit and he was too slow. The net twisted again. Then it wrapped itself around the crane arm in a tight ball of mesh.

'Damn it.' Bruce managed to get the hoist turned off. Then he stared at the net in dismay. It looked like a serious mission to untangle it. Bruce felt the deck shake beneath his feet as the ship's engines rumbled into life.

112

Tehpoe had, like Gwen, been thrown into one of the squalid shacks that littered Commander Kickback's camp. The ten-year-old boy was in shock, still groggy from his illness and now in the grip of a morbid sense of dread.

Captured by the notorious Captain Kickback.

Tehpoe had heard the stories of what Kickback made his boy soldiers do. Images of mutilation and torture tormented the child as he stood there quivering with fear in the stinking little cell.

Tehpoe had lost his mother and father in a rebel attack by a similar band of desperadoes; the village had been ransacked, his home burned to the ground. Only when his father had pushed him towards the forest and urged him to run for his life had he managed to escape the mayhem.

Now, Tehpoe made the most difficult decision of his young life. He could either lie down and accept his terrible fate.

Or he could try and escape.

Tehpoe crossed to the doorway and peeked through the splintered planks. A young soldier had been detailed to guard him but Tehpoe could see now that he was so drugged he had fallen into a deep sleep. Through his spyhole Tehpoe could see that some of Kickback's men were sitting nearby, smoking and drinking, but one by one they seemed to be passing out, or crawling to a nearby shelter to sleep. They had been marching for days and were dog tired.

He thought about Gwen, wondering where they had taken her. The Australian had been so kind to Tehpoe that he knew he could not leave without at least trying to help her.

After a while the camp was completely quiet.

113

John and Fran Hicks waited until the last of the protestors had filed past. The Mercedes limousine then slipped away from the Cosmos Hotel and into the streets of the capital.

During their wait the driver had persuaded them it would be better to head out of town for the day and the Australian couple had agreed to head to Bagar—a Buddhist complex of exquisite golden shrines which Fran had long wanted to see and photograph.

The chauffeur took a side road at the first opportunity, heading away from the demonstration down a potholed section of track which passed several shuttered up government buildings.

'This short cut will avoid the People's Park,' he told his passengers. 'Then we can leave the city.'

But as they rounded a bend in the road they saw the end of the route was blocked. An intimidating row of grey-painted battle tanks was sitting there, surrounded by government troops. The young soldiers stared at the de luxe vehicle with ill disguised contempt and for the first time John and Fran felt disconcerted. The atmosphere in the streets was definitely deteriorating.

There was no one else around. It seemed the whole town had gone to ground with the exception of the military and the monks.

'I don't think these guys are very happy to see us,' Fran said.

Her husband merely grunted. He'd travelled the world several times over in his lifetime and he wasn't about to be fazed by a bunch of ramboed up teenagers even if they did have some serious firepower at their command.

'Let's try another route please, driver.'

114

Todd and Isabella were still sitting on their precarious branch above the side pool of the Jari river. The minutes and hours were creeping by but Todd knew they had a long way to go before dawn. The young Australian felt he had never known time to drag so painfully. Mosquitos and other biting insects of the night were flocking to feed on them.

The gringo and the local girl were keeping absolutely still, their muscles cramped and protesting under the continued effort to avoid putting the branch under more stress.

Even so, the branch would let out an occasional crack as it bent ever more under their combined weight. It had sagged so much that Todd's lower legs were dangling in the river. There was no other branch they could move to; Todd had already checked that out.

Todd switched on his headtorch. He was conserving the power to try and protect the battery. Five minutes every hour.

That was when he felt a sharp jabbing pain on his calf. Todd jerked his leg back in a reflex reaction.

'Ow!' he exclaimed, shocked at the intense pain and wondering immediately if he had been bitten by a snake. He raised his leg, seeing a curiously circular hole just a centimetre in diameter. Todd stared at it closely, seeing that his flesh was stamped with a neat row of clearly defined teeth marks.

He shone his torch into the pool below them and—just for an instant—caught a flash of scaly silver as a fish darted out of sight.

One word flashed into his mind a split second later.

Piranha.

115

The Hicks's driver did a hasty turn and drove swiftly back to the main road. The way back to the hotel was filled with advancing soldiers. He took a right and immediately had to brake hard as a convoy of military jeeps swept across the route at high speed. Each one was packed with more of the stony-faced militia, their assault rifles to the ready.

'I think it's time to go back to the hotel,' Fran told her husband.

'No, no,' Hicks told her impatiently, 'we're not going to let some bunch of toy soldiers spoil our day. We said we're going to the temples at Bagar so that's where we're going. Let's see if we can find another route.'

'I think she is right, sir,' the chauffeur chipped in nervously. 'This is not the day to be on the . . . '

'Nonsense, man,' Hicks snorted. 'Let's keep driving and we'll find a way through.'

The driver consulted a city map on his lap for a moment and then accelerated away down a street lined with shops which were all shuttered up. Within a short distance they came to a grinding halt once more as they encountered another huge column of monks marching towards the People's Park.

The holy men seemed curious about the occupants of the luxury car, many of them pausing to take a good look at who was inside. With hundreds of the protestors pressing against the vehicle the Hickses' feeling of vulnerability was growing.

'Don't show any fear,' Hicks muttered to his wife.

They waved uneasily to the monks who then walked on.

'This demonstration is going to be very big,' the driver said, 'I have never seen so many monks out on the streets, the soldiers are not going to like it.'

116

The double shot Americano had done Marko no favours at all. The caffeine had wired him up completely and he began to realize that he might be experiencing a delayed form of shock from the dramas of the morning. His palms were clammy with sweat, his hands shaking with a perceptible tremor. An intense hot spot of pain began to form in the middle of his forehead.

He walked to Belmore Park and sat on a bench in the shade. But there were dozens of butterflies skipping about the flowers and he found himself scrutinizing them closely.

Was that the one? It certainly looked like it.

That was when Marko made a snap decision. He decided he needed a bit of a work-out, a distraction from these troubling thoughts. He flipped open his mobile and dialled his girlfriend. 'I'm thinking of going down to the harbour,' Marko told Denise. 'Do a bit of a session with the Dragon Boat guys.'

'That's a weekend thing, isn't it? You never go in the weekdays.' Denise's voice was just a fraction of a degree above absolute zero.

'Yeah, I know. But I need some exercise, Den. After the morning I've had . . . '

'Whatever.' Denise slammed down the phone.

Marko took the light railway down to the port, disembarking at the Pyrmont Bay stop and making his way to the small waterside shack which was home to the Sydney

Dragon Boat team. Five or six of the guys were already there, preparing the boat, and Marko got some warm greetings from his mates.

'You in the mood for a work-out, Marko?'

'You bet I am.'

117

Captain Olberg checked his watch. They were already well over the projected departure time. And all because of that stupid van.

Little by little the tide would be turning, rising millimetre by millimetre as the minutes ticked by, every further delay making the transit out of the harbour more perilous.

'How are we doing?' he asked the officer of the watch.

'Not so bad, sir. That's the last of the passengers on board.'

'Thank God for that. What about the cargo?'

'Almost done, sir.'

'Good. Let me know the moment we can sail.'

Olberg was itching to get the *Cayman Glory* underway. He had already put out a radio call to alert Ella Andersen, the duty pilot, that he wanted her on board at the earliest opportunity to supervise the ship's departure from Sydney.

He walked quickly to the observation platform above the rear cargo area to check out progress on the loading. Straight away he saw the mess of netting wrapped around the crane.

'What's going on with that net?' he called down.

'It's snagged, sir,' Bruce replied.

'Well, unsnag it as quick as you can!'

'Yes, sir.'

Olberg turned abruptly, and made his way quickly up to the bridge. Honestly, he thought, today it really is just one thing after another with this port turnaround.

It was going to be wonderful, Olberg mused, to be sailing away from all this into the open ocean.

He entered the bridge and snapped a command.

'Radio the pilot again, please. Urgently. We need her on board asap.'

118

Marko went to his locker and changed into his sport gear. He was already starting to feel a bit more like himself and the headache was starting to ease.

The security guard always got a buzz when he went to the Dragon Boat club; there was a tight sense of camaraderie between the members, the shared sense of sporting endeavour coupled with some hilarious characters and the knowledge that no matter how hard the training session the beers in the bar afterwards would more than compensate.

The Dragon Boat was constructed from fibreglass, the shape of the hull copied from two-thousand-year-old designs of the original boats that competed on the Chiang Ziang river to celebrate the summer rice harvest.

Now, Marko greeted a few familiar faces and took a seat in the front of the boat. He was one of the pacers—the role reserved for the most experienced paddlers of all, and the ones who set the stroke for the other twenty paddlers in the craft.

In front of him was the drummer, another tradition taken from the Chinese origins of the sport. His job was to watch the pacers like a hawk, varying the timing of his drum strokes to match them, and motivating the crew to hit the mark.

The boat was eased away from the pier. The pacers dug their paddles in at a leisurely speed. No need for serious effort yet, much better to loosen up the muscles and have a good stretch as the boat headed out into the harbour.

Marko felt the stress of the day melting away as the team got into the rhythm. It was good to be out on the water.

119

Tammy Simons and Murray West were preparing for their first hit on the *Cayman Glory*.

For Tammy this meant retreating to the lavatory and putting on a dark wig and some thick-rimmed glasses. For Murray it was just a matter of wheeling himself into the restaurant.

Even though the vessel had not yet set sail, the all-day buffet had already opened for the new passengers. Vast serving stations were dishing out roast meats, barbecued prawns, and spaghetti dishes as fast as they could be cooked.

Murray scanned the room: he knew exactly what he was looking for. An elderly passenger. A woman ideally. And most certainly dining alone at one of the communal tables.

There. The perfect mark. A rather sweet, slightly dazed looking lady picking delicately at a salad at a corner table. She had to be eighty if she was a day.

She was dripping with diamonds. Her handbag was placed on the seat to her side.

Not that she would be paying much attention to it; Murray and Tammy had learned many years before that the 'closed world' environment of a cruise ship fosters a very trusting attitude.

No one imagines a theft can happen at sea.

Murray queued up for a couple of big pieces of pizza and a Coke. Placing the tray on his lap, he wheeled himself across the restaurant to the old lady's table.

'Mind if I sit here?' he asked politely.

'Why of course,' the elderly lady replied.

She pulled a chair aside so that Murray could get his wheelchair close to the table.

120

Ella Andersen tucked her pilot's log under her arm and ran up the passenger gangway onto the *Cayman Glory*. Even as she reached the top of the metal ramp the stevedores were already unfastening the metal fixings which held the ramp in place. The hydraulic rams would soon be pulling the bridgeway back onto shore, freeing the vessel to leave port.

Time was ticking away, and Ella had already been warned by a senior colleague that the ship was running dangerously late to get under the Sydney Harbour Bridge before the tide rose. It was her reponsibility as the duty pilot to ensure that the ship's departure would be a safe one, so her stress levels were running high to say the least.

Ella was greeted in the passenger muster area by the officer of the watch who took her immediately to the forward lift and then on onto the bridge where Captain Stian Olberg was waiting for her.

'Heard you had a little scrape with a truck,' Ella told him. Word of the lobster van incident had already spread all over the harbour.

'Damn nuisance,' Olberg snapped. 'Lost us an hour. Now I need to take your advice on the question of the tide.'

Ella took out her pilot's log and flipped to the back of the book. This was where the crucial high and low tides were marked for each day of the month, along with precise (at least to the minute) timings for the same. She checked her watch and made some calculations on her PDA. Then she checked it again, just to be doubly safe.

'We can do it,' she told Olberg. 'with two metres to spare, but we have to pass beneath the bridge in the next fifteen minutes.'

121

Tehpoe had waited long enough.

Now he stood up quietly and crossed to the window of the fetid little shack. Through the bars he could get a view of the 'parade ground', illuminated by moonlight.

There was no movement. All was dead quiet. Even the creatures of the jungle had stopped their nocturnal serenade. Now was the perfect moment to make a move but it took a monumental act of courage for the ten-year-old child to make the decision to act.

Tehpoe went to the door and pushed it gently. He felt the resistance as the door hit the comatose body of the guard. The boy soldier mumbled a bit but didn't get anywhere near waking as Tehpoe opened the door with more force.

Tehpoe was out. He stepped over the guard and melted into the shadows of the nearby trees where he waited for some minutes to satisfy himself that no one had seen him leave the shack.

The temptation to cut and run was almost irresistible. Tehpoe knew he could survive for a couple of days in the jungle, felt sure he could reach a road if he just kept moving. But that would be a betrayal. Just the thought of what might happen to Gwen when Kickback found he had escaped was enough to convince Tehpoe to start his search for her.

Now he started moving across the camp, picking his footfalls with infinite care so he didn't inadvertently crack a branch underfoot.

'Pssst!' Telipoe heard the low hiss and turned towards a nearby shack. Through the bars on the window he could see Gwen staring out at him. He silently walked over.

122

Fifteen minutes. Olberg checked the chart on the desk in front of him. They could make it—at a pinch.

Ella had given him all the information; she'd done her job as a pilot to the utmost of her ability and she was absolutely sure that her assessment was correct. But the final decision on whether or not to take the risk would be down to Olberg—as the captain of the vessel.

Olberg felt the pressure of the decision weighing down on him acutely. It went against the grain to take even the slightest risk with the *Cayman Glory*. An impact with the Harbour Bridge would mean disaster for the ship and its passengers, not to mention the end of Olberg's career and a possible repair bill for millions of dollars.

But an extra night in port would cost the owner of the vessel dear, and create other complications later on the cruise. No one would be thanking Olberg for his prudent decision-making if he ducked out of the risk and took the safe option.

What was more, the pilot had given her professional judgement that they had a good two metres of headroom. They would have to leave immediately and make all speed.

'Cast off the mooring lines fore and aft,' Olberg snapped to the officer of the watch. 'We leave right away.'

123

Today's session in the Dragon Boat was a familiar routine for Marko and his mates; a 'warm-up' paddle out into the harbour then a timed work-out under the watchful eye of the Dragon Boat team manager Paul Masters who accompanied them in his inflatable Zodiac.

The time trial could never replicate the blood and thunder of a real race, of course, but Marko relished the prospect of the intense physical activity.

Apart from anything else it would help him forget about the morning's events back at the tower block.

'All right, boys,' Paul Masters was yelling at them from the Zodiac, 'let's pick the pace up, shall we?'

Marko felt his biceps tingle as the crew upped the energy input. His whole body felt energized and fit. It was a beautiful Sydney afternoon, the city looking clean and fresh beneath a cloudless sky.

A ship's siren blasted off over by the cruise ship berths.

'Big one going out,' Marko commented to his mate.

Soon the elegant vessel was steaming past the tiny Dragon Boat. It passed by so closely that Marko could see the name: the *Cayman Glory*. Passengers were waving to them from the decks.

Marko lifted his arm and gave them a friendly wave back.

No doubt about it, Marko thought, that's a hell of a good-looking ship.

124

As soon as he had himself positioned at the table Murray
West turned to the elderly lady.

'I have a bit of trouble with my hands,' Murray told
her. 'Would you be kind enough to cut up my pizza for
me?'

'It would be a pleasure.' No one ever refused. How could
they?

Cutting a healthy sized pizza into small pieces is a fair
amount of work. It takes a minute and a half to two
minutes on average (Tammy and Murray had timed it on
many occasions).

During that time, Tammy made her move.

She crossed the restaurant with her tray (loaded with
nothing more than a yoghurt and a bowl of fruit) and took
the seat on the other side of the elderly woman.

She got the line of approach absolutely right. Right in
the blind spot. The elderly woman had her back turned to
Tammy, and was only vaguely aware of her presence. She
certainly hadn't had a good look at her face. Murray kept a
line of patter going with the elderly lady, talking about how
excited he was to be taking the cruise, as Tammy prepared
for the hit.

At the crucial moment Murray knocked his knife and
fork off the table. He did it in such a way that they fell
beneath and behind his wheelchair.

'Butter fingers,' Murray smiled apologetically, 'would you mind picking those back up for me?'

'But of course!' The elderly lady kindly reached down to pick up the dropped cutlery.

In that instant Tammy slipped the handbag into her hand. She clicked open the clasp and deftly sorted through the belongings until she found the purse.

125

The small circular wound in Todd's calf was dripping blood into the river. Isabella's head wound was, from time to time, doing the same. 'Close your eyes,' Todd told the girl. He wanted to check out the water beneath them and he didn't want her any more freaked out than she already was.

He turned on the torch and saw movement beneath the surface of the river. Reflected in the light of the headtorch there was a shimmering, glass-like ripple of light. It was mesmerizing, really rather beautiful.

That single piranha had been joined by hundreds more.

'Meu Deus!' Isabella cried. She hadn't been able to resist a quick look.

Piranhas are opportunistic hunters, aggressive fish which school and feed en masse; their interlocking teeth are designed to shear and rip skin with devastating efficiency. Legend has it that a few thousand of these voracious creatures can strip the flesh off a fully grown horse in less than a minute, reducing it to a skeleton with terrifying ease.

Todd certainly wasn't going to argue with that; the one small bite on his calf was enough to convince him.

Todd shifted position to ease his aching muscles, the branch creaking ominously as their combined weight tested its limits.

'Oh, man . . .' Todd groaned in despair as a fresh drop of blood hit the river, the piranhas snapping and twisting crazily in the water beneath them.

Todd knew now that their survival would depend on one thing: how long could that spindly section of branch support their weight?

'Keep still,' he told Isabella, 'don't move a muscle.'

126

Tammy quickly opened up the purse, finding a stiff little wad of fifty dollar bills. Just on this quick glimpse she could tell there was upwards of three thousand dollars there. She plucked out about two thirds of the cash and placed it in her pocket. This was a crucial part of the strategy—i.e., not to take it all.

If the old lady reported it as a crime then she would surely be disbelieved. What thief would *leave* some of the money? People would be more inclined to think she had mis-counted, or absent mindedly misplaced the cash.

Tammy put the purse back in the bag and slipped it back into position just as the lady bobbed back up with Murray's cutlery triumphantly in her hand.

By the time the old lady had finished cutting Murray's pizza up, Tammy had discreetly slipped away from the table and the hit was done. Tammy left the restaurant at a leisurely pace. There was nothing whatsoever about her demeanour to suggest she had just relieved a fellow passenger of more than two thousand US dollars in cash.

Suddenly the ship's tannoy blurted into life: 'Ladies and gentlemen, we are now setting sail. That means the casino is now open on deck three if you feel in the mood for a flutter.'

Tammy checked a map of the ship's layout, then took

elevator seven up to the entertainment deck. She was alone in the lift so she took off the wig and glasses and placed them in her bag. Moments later she was entering the gaudy environment of the *Cayman Glory*'s casino which was already busy with punters.

Tammy loved to gamble. Specially with other people's money.

127

The star was what is known as a *Main Sequence Star*, that is to say, the type which generates energy through the nuclear fusion of hydrogen nuclei into helium. This one was orbiting in the Orion arm of the Milky Way Galaxy, just one of over one hundred million similar stars which are dotted in seemingly random fashion through that particular region of space.

Here on Earth we call it the Sun.

In the heart of that celestial orb, with every passing second, more than four million tons of matter was being converted by the processes of fusion into neutrinos and solar radiation. These spill in unimaginable quantities into the vacuum of space and begin a journey of one hundred and forty-nine million kilometres to the tiny, blue, orbiting planet that we call home.

It takes eight minutes and nineteen seconds to make it to Earth at a speed of 299,792 kilometres a second. This is the speed of light moving through a vacuum.

If the rays had happened to strike the Earth on a patch of ocean, or a sandy piece of desert floor, they would have had little impact beyond transferring their energy in the form of heat. But this particular shaft of sunlight did not fall harmlessly to the surface of our planet. The rays happened to strike a fragment of glass which was stuck in a huge firework sitting in a newly opened cardboard box high above Sydney Harbour Bridge . . .

The lozenge of glass now acted as a magnifying glass; the sunlight concentrated into a single pencil point of high energy, and considerable heat.

Directly beneath the piece of glass, the densely packed firework began to smoke as the casing began to burn through.

128

General Pauk Taw could sense that the mood of the crowd had soured. Parading the young monk and his radio in front of the crowd had been a provocation too far.

'Free him!' the monks chorused. 'Free our brother!'

General Pauk Taw screamed into his megaphone for them to stop but his screeching, electronically distorted voice had no effect other than to cause the monks to shout even louder. Some were even yelling anti-government slogans, an offence which was punishable by life imprisonment or even a death penalty.

Pauk Taw ordered the water cannons to be opened up again. The plumes of water rained down on the demonstrators but the shock value was lost now and the monks had become adept at dodging out of the way.

'Baton charge!' was his next command. A phalanx of troops rushed into the demonstrators and began to beat those at the front. But the demonstrators had put their sturdiest men in the first line of fire and many of them were martial arts experts.

Some of the soldiers had their batons wrestled from them.

When the charge came it took General Pauk Taw and his men completely by surprise. As if by some secret signal, the thousands of monks rose to their feet with a tremendous roar. Banners and the occasional stone rained down on the soldiers and they responded with volleys of gunfire, aimed high above the demonstrators' heads.

The crowd rushed towards the military line, leaving the general no time to issue orders to his nervy young troops.

Seconds later a full scale riot was under way.

129

CASINO: THE *CAYMAN GLORY*

The casino was cleverly designed to resemble a theme park with its pirate displays, elaborate fountains and tanks filled with exotic tropical fish. The objective was to instil an atmosphere of relaxed sophisticated fun.

Tammy went straight to the bar.

'I'll take a champagne cocktail,' she told the bartender. 'With a dash of bitters.' The bartender did the business and Tammy took her drink with her as she walked around the casino.

Then she noticed the strongroom.

Tammy took a keen look, her criminal interest piqued as ever when it came to assessing the security measures of places which routinely handled large sums of cash. This one was like many others she had seen: effectively a metal cage built within the confines of an office and with a substantial old-fashioned style steel safe sitting in one corner.

Inside the strongroom she could see the casino safe was open. Two cashiers were loading it up with neat bricks of hundred dollar notes. Tammy felt her pulse quicken as she saw the mountain of cash. More than a million, she felt sure.

Now that really would be worth a risk.

One day, she promised herself in a brief mental note, she really must talk to Murray about pulling off a big one. Hitting on old ladies for a couple of thousand here and there was effective but time consuming.

How much better would it be to score a hit that was big enough to keep them in luxury for the rest of their lives? The very thought of it made Tammy giddy with excitement. She watched the strongroom carefully as she sipped her cocktail.

130

John Hicks grunted with exasperation as the chauffeured Mercedes came—yet again—to a halt. Another roadblock had been erected in front of them, a row of solid concrete blocks which were quite impossible to move.

Hicks could feel a painful tightness embracing his chest. He loosened his collar a bit to get some more air but the taut feeling continued and he could see shiny stars floating in front of his vision. Suddenly he realized that his arm was feeling numb. He tried flexing his fingers but they seemed now strangely disconnected to the rest of his body.

'Our tour is over.' the chauffeur said. 'There's no way out of town.'

Fran was on the driver's side. 'Darling, I really do think it's time to go back to the . . . '

'All right!' Hicks finally agreed. 'Enough is enough. Let's get the hell out of here.' He was interrupted by the sound of screams and sirens coming from the square.

'Oh my God.' Fran was the first to see the hundreds of monks who were now running down the street towards them. Behind the terrified protestors a wall of armour was hailing down water and tear gas on the fleeing crowd.

The chauffeur hit the accelerator hard, spinning the car wildly and shooting off down a narrow alley which was now their only escape route back to the hotel.

Now the monks were running alongside the vehicle, sprinting for their lives as the military pursuit entered the alley behind them. A few baton rounds of rubber bullets smacked into the men as they ran.

Something hit the back window of the vehicle, shattering it instantly.

131

Just past midnight local time the branch broke.

Even though they had feared it for hours, the actual moment took Todd and Isabella completely by surprise. One second they were sitting side by side on the branch, the next there was a huge *crack* and they found themselves falling waist deep into the water. In the next instant the two of them were subjected to the most excruciating assault as many dozens of piranhas went into attack mode.

'Aieeegh!' Todd let out an involuntary scream as the predators set about him. Instinctively, his hands moved down into the water, to beat at the attackers, but there were too many by far and the only result was that his hands took upwards of a dozen fast bites from the frenzied piranhas.

'Help me!' the girl screamed. He grabbed hold of Isabella and lifted her up and out of the water. Even as he did so he could see the flash of quicksilver on her legs as the predators continued their attack.

Todd splashed through the water and reached the wall of mud which flanked the pool. He lifted Isabella higher so she could grab hold of a thick root which was sticking out of the bank above them. Then he hauled himself up out of the water by grasping the same root. He kicked his trainers into the muddy wall, creating a little shelf with the side of his feet.

How long they could hold on to this desperate position he had no idea. They were both bleeding heavily from the bites.

Then Todd heard an engine out on the river.

'I see a light!' Isabella cried.

The two of them began to scream for help.

132

The *Cayman Glory* was steaming at full speed for the Harbour Bridge, Captain Stian Olberg next to the officer of the watch and Ella Andersen, the Sydney Harbour service pilot, right by his side.

Tension was high amongst all those present. The critical moment was just a couple of minutes away, the moment the ship would slip beneath the bridge—or (if Ella had got her sums wrong on the tides) lose its radio mast in the process and put a dent in the bridge which could close it for days or even weeks.

And it wasn't just the radio mast that would be damaged. The tubular steel structure of the ship's high point was also rigged with wiring for the radar sender unit, and was stuffed with electronics responsible for the on-board GPS and navigation systems. Each one of these was a custom built entity in its own right, designed for the *Cayman Glory* and the *Cayman Glory* alone.

Even the slightest damage would mean a return to port and a series of time consuming repairs. Specialists would have to be summoned from the various countries from which the systems were sourced.

Olberg felt his mouth horribly dry. He sipped on the dregs of a cold cup of coffee to wet his lips.

As they approached the bridge they could see the huge

metal fireworks gantry that had been winched into position high on the superstructure.

'They say it's going to be the biggest fireworks display Sydney's ever seen,' the officer of the watch commented.

Olberg merely grunted a reply; he was too wrapped up in the passage out of the harbour to reply.

133

The light that Todd and Isabella had seen belonged to a river smuggler by the name of Thiago and he was at that moment making his way up the Jari river in his motorized canoe.

Thiago always took to the river at the dead of night when—he hoped—the police, the campesinos and their families would be safely asleep in their shacks.

A lifetime navigating in the dark hours had given him supersensitive night vision, and he could pick his way through even the most complicated rapids with just a feeble light on the front of his canoe. Now he heard a man's shout from the bank: 'Help! Help us, please!' Then a girl's voice screaming the same in the local language.

Thiago was perplexed and not a little unnerved. He knew there were no cabins on that part of the bend, and that the banks there were inaccessible at best.

He frowned, figuring it might be a police trap. He had an illegal cargo of gold dust on board and a stolen consignment of antibiotics. The police had been hunting for him for years and they were cunning enough to try anything.

The smuggler suspected that the cries were designed to lure him into the bank where he would meet a hail of bullets. He had survived numerous similar scares in the past.

'Please! For the love of God!' the girl screamed.

Thiago felt his conscience pricked; the girl certainly sounded genuinely terrified. But he had too much to lose and he didn't want to get involved.

He quickly turned his canoe round and headed back to Porto Velho where he knew a corrupt port official who would guard his canoe. He would take a drink in a bar and try the rapids again later.

134

Tehpoe's heart was beating so hard he felt sure that it would wake up everyone in the camp. His mouth was so dry with terror that he could barely swallow as he crossed to the shack where Gwen was being held captive.

There was a guard slumped on a chair not far from the door of the shack. He seemed blind drunk, or drugged out of his skull, and his ageing Kalashnikov rifle had fallen to the ground at his feet.

Tehpoe inched forward, making his way along the wall of the shack until he reached the barred window where Gwen was waiting. The young boy kept a wary eye on the snoring guard. If he woke, he would see him in an instant.

It took a moment for his eyes to adjust to the dark interior of the shack, but he could see Gwen's gleaming eyes, wet with tears. She reached through the bars and grasped Tehpoe's hand with a fierce grip.

'What are you doing?' she whispered. 'You can't let them see you here.'

'I want to get you out,' he whispered back.

Gwen shook her head. 'It's too risky. Save yourself, Tehpoe. Run away, as fast as you can.'

'No.' Tehpoe turned away and paced along the wall to the door. He could see immediately that it was solid and well built. He turned the handle slowly but the lock seemed firm.

Then he looked over at the drunken guard. On his belt he could see a glint of metal, illuminated by the moonlight. It was a key.

135

Ella bit down hard on her lip. It was going to be so damn *tight*.

Through the glass section of the roof of the bridge they could see the mast towering directly above them.

Then they were through.

With a metre and a half of air between the top of the mast and the base of the bridge.

'Yes!' The officer of the watch shouted a cry of relief.

Captain Stian Olberg let out a long breath.

'That was as close as I like it to be,' he said. 'But I think we made the right call.'

He held his hand out to Ella and she shook it with considerable relief.

'Nice work, Ella,' he congratulated her. Ella smiled modestly, happy to take the praise even though the handshake had reminded her painfully of the wounds in her palms.

The crew looked ahead. Out into the open ocean where whitecaps were playing on the waves.

No one looked back where hell was about to break loose.

For whilst it was true that the highest point of the *Cayman Glory* had passed beneath the bridge, there was still plenty more of the vessel to come.

More than one hundred and fifty metres of the superstructure still had to pass beneath it.

136

The bar was the *Rio Grande,* a dubious neon-lit establish-
ment in the heart of the seediest district of Porto Velho. It
boasted a scuffed-up pool table with two broken cues and a
television with more static than picture but Thiago felt at
home here, his craggy features fitting in well with the tired
ladies of the night and hard-drinking river men who drifted
into the town looking for labouring jobs.

The bar owner greeted Thiago with a hearty shout
of 'Amigo!' and a sweaty hug. Everybody profited when
Thiago was about; and his smuggling exploits had won him
a certain reputation amongst the poor of the Jari river as a
sort of latter day Robin Hood.

Thiago downed his shot in a single swift movement,
relishing the kick as the alcohol coursed rapidly through
his body. He was thinking about that bizarre incident out
on the river. Those strange shouts that had come out of
the riverbank.

He was feeling angry with himself. Perhaps it hadn't
been the police after all? Maybe the cries had been genuine?

Thiago took another glass of the coarse liquor, taking
his time on this one as he watched the twenty-four hour
news channel on the ancient television. Then the sudden
sound of thunder rent the air.

The metallic thrumming of rain on the corrugated iron
roof of the bar announced a downpour.

137

Shaun was aware that a huge cruise ship was passing beneath the bridge. But he couldn't afford to be distracted now. He reached into box number forty-three and grabbed at the last of the fireworks, the rounded 'maroon' or flash-bomb which contained more than a kilo of black powder and a substantial quantity of titanium.

Shaun stared at the smoking firework, not sure he could believe what he was seeing. The maroon was definitely smouldering. But what had caused such a thing to happen?

Shaun twisted his body so he could see the back of the firework. Straight away he saw the shard of glass which was embedded in the body of the device. At the same instant he saw the hole that the focused rays of the sun had burned into the shell.

With a jolt of fear he realized he had to pluck the glass out fast or the flash powder could detonate.

He was reaching for the shard as the powder went off.

The blast hit Shaun full in the face from a distance of approximately twenty centimetres. Shaun's world went rainbow bright. But only for a split millisecond before:

The propulsive force of the detonation turned his face virtually inside out. His jaw bone, teeth and both cheek bones were immediately blown back into the deepest recess of his brain.

At that point it would be safe to say Shaun's day took a discernible turn for the worst.

He slumped back stone dead against the metal frame, the winch control unit still clutched in his hand. His thumb was locked on the unit. The winch was still pulling up on the gantry.

138

Tehpoe crept forwards on his hands and knees until he was poised just an arm's length from the sleeping guard. Seen from this intimate viewpoint the warrior was a truly depraved sight, his patchy uniform decorated with voodoo fetishes.

By the silvery moonlight Tehpoe could see what looked like a monkey's withered hand pinned on the man's chest. At least he hoped it was a monkey's hand. The soldier's mouth was wide open as he snored in his drunken stupor and Tehpoe noticed with horror that his teeth were filed sharp—a tradition amongst those rebels who had a taste for human flesh.

He could see the key, attached to a cord which had been slipped through the guy's belt.

Tehpoe steeled himself and reached forward, tentatively grabbing the key and giving it a small tug to see how firmly it was fixed. Then he stopped, drawing his hand back as the guard snored loudly. Tehpoe was horribly aware that if the guard woke up he would probably shoot him right away.

He tried again, this time managing to move the key so that he could check out the knot that was holding it. He was in luck, the drunken guard had tied it in place with the simplest of overhand knots. Tehpoe managed to untie it and now he had the key in his hand.

He crossed to the door but the lock was rusty. The key didn't seem to fit. Tehpoe went through an agonizing minute as he tried to get it to work.

'Give it to me here,' Gwen hissed from the window, 'I'll try it from inside.' A few seconds later, Tehpoe heard the scraping metal sound of the lock yielding to the key. Then Gwen was out of her prison and taking his hand.

They started to make their way across the parade ground, heading for the cover of the surrounding forest.

139

High above the vessel, the gantry winch—unable to stop with Shaun's hand jammed on the switch—was winding itself into melting point.

The winch began to strain as the motor smoked under the pressure. Shaun's colleague spun in his harness, trying with all his might to reach the handset which would enable him to turn it off. But the handset was completely jammed behind the gantry, with the pressure of many tonnes of steel holding it in place.

The winch kept grinding as it pulled at the steel cable.

An instant later, the winch blew itself to smithereens. The steel cable whipped back as it broke, sending the entire north end of the gantry into freefall as it swung loose, complete with its load of fireworks. Shaun's colleague plummeted with it, slamming into the steel girder twenty metres below him and dying instantly of multiple trauma.

The gantry swung in a great arc, ripping out the guide ropes as it went. The end smashed into the support pylons of the harbour bridge as it reached a perfectly vertical position.

For a moment it hung there, motionless, held in place by just a single attachment. But the one hundred and fifty tonne steel structure was too much for the single welded bracket to hold. It strained, then buckled . . .

And then it snapped.

The gantry plummeted like a giant spear towards the rear deck of the *Cayman Glory*.

140

Wai Yan covered his ears as the demonstrators began to beat on the metal walls of the armoured car. The thunderous noise created by hundreds of fists was deafening.

He could hear muffled commands from the military. Through the window he could see the general who had arrested him. The man was screaming blue murder into his megaphone but the troops around him had lost control, overwhelmed by sheer numbers.

A monk was trying to smash the armoured car window with a rock. But the glass was obviously bullet proof and he couldn't breach it.

Then Wai Yan felt the vehicle rock. The rioters had started to push at the sides.

'They're going to kill us!' the guard screamed.

Finally the armoured car toppled onto its side. Wai Yan was airborne for a split second before crashing heavily into the guard. The man pushed him away with some difficulty, uttering swear words which were the worst the young monk had ever heard. The crowd was still beating on the metal shell as the winded soldier crawled over to unlock the door.

Wai Yan felt a dozen hands grab hold of him. He was pulled out of the vehicle and helped to his feet. The guard was getting kicked as he tried to crawl away from the scene.

'Leave him!' Wai Yan shouted, trying to protect the man. A grenade blasted nearby. A thick cloud of orange smoke began to engulf the protestors as nearby troops prepared to charge them.

Wai Yan took his chance. He picked up his robes and ran.

141

The fireworks gantry smashed vertically through the glass atrium roof of the *Cayman Glory*, showering the shoppers in the on board mall below with many thousands of pieces of shattered glass as the massive metal structure fell four storeys in less than a heartbeat, as straight as an arrow, to the floor below.

It happened so fast that most were unable to comprehend what was happening. Passengers screamed as clothes and flesh were ripped beneath the cascade of razor sharp pieces.

The gantry hit the floor, but it didn't stop there. It had too much mass and was travelling too fast to be stopped by the lightweight aluminium panels on top of the lift bay. So it ripped a path right through, splitting lift number fourteen wide open and free-falling down the lift shaft which opened up below.

Lift shafts are notorious weak spots in the structural make up of a vessel such as the *Cayman Glory*. Ships' architects know they have to incorporate them, but they seriously compromise certain aspects of the superstructure's integrity—being in effect a hole which passes from top to bottom.

This was the biggest lift shaft on the ship. Plenty of room for the invading gantry to continue its journey.

The metal gantry fell eight storeys down the lift shaft and slammed into the final floor of the ship, a non-load-bearing metal surface just one eighteenth of an inch thick. The impact was fast and decisive. the steel gantry immediately punching a hole in the welded plates and penetrating the cavity below.

A cavity containing fuel bunker number six.

And that was when the fireworks really started.

142

The Mercedes was travelling at about fifty kilometres an hour when it hit Wai Yan. The boy was running at full tilt down an adjacent road and the chauffeur never stood a chance of avoiding him when he ran out in front of the car.

The near-side wing hit the novice monk square on the thigh, the impact throwing him a metre or so in the air, bowling him over in a cloud of yellow dust.

John and Fran Hicks climbed from the vehicle. Other protestors were running past them, paying no heed to the injured boy who lay unconscious in the dust.

'Is he alive?' Fran asked, her voice cracking with emotion as her husband knelt to try and find a pulse.

'He's alive. But this leg is broken for sure.'

143

The explosion sent a shock wave rippling through the vessel. The *Cayman Glory* shuddered with the violence of the blow. Captain Olberg steadied himself as the vessel rocked, then he turned and saw the blue/black plume of smoke pouring in serious quantities out of the atrium area.

For a few moments Captain Olberg was speechless with shock. How had such a thing happened? A bomb? A terrorist attack with an aircraft?

'Engines to full reverse!' he ordered. 'Activate the sprinkler system.'

Olberg waited to hear the telltale sound of the engines winding down. It was imperative to slow the vessel before it reached deeper water. But no such thing was happening.

'Put out a mayday call. Muster the passengers on the lifeboat deck,' Olberg ordered. 'I'm going down to the engine room to see why they're not responding.'

144

The crew of the Sydney Harbour Dragon Boat heard the *whoomph* of the explosion as they hit the four hundred metre mark on their training run.

'Pull . . . pull . . . ' The caller's cries petered out as he saw the evil looking black smoke pouring out of the back of the cruise ship. The Zodiac carrying team boss Paul Masters pulled up alongside them. 'Session's over,' he told the stunned crew of the Dragon Boat, 'I'm going to take the Zodiac over and see if we can help.'

'I'm coming with you,' Marko said.

Masters made a snap decision; he knew Marko was a qualified life saver, he was the right man to have in the Zodiac at this moment. 'OK.' He held out his hand and helped Marko to jump into the inflatable.

Then he turned into the swell, giving the engine some power as the five metre Zodiac headed for the stricken ship.

145

Gwen grabbed Tehpoe's hand and pulled him as fast as she could across the clearing which doubled as a parade ground.

The mutilated bodies of the three government soldiers were still lying were they had fallen, and Gwen had to fight the urge to retch as the nauseating stench of decomposing flesh hit her.

Suddenly there was a loud barking from one of the shacks. One of the dogs seemed to have sensed that something was wrong and now the other joined it in a competition to see which could howl and snarl the loudest.

If those dogs wake the rebels, Gwen thought, we won't stand a chance.

Thirty metres to go. The welcoming embrace of the forest was so close.

146

Captain Olberg and his first officer ran from the bridge and took the forward stairway. In the lower decks all was noise and mayhem. Passengers were fighting, coughing, and spluttering their way through the fumes, some even carrying their bags.

'Leave your bags in the cabins!' Olberg shouted.

He was wasting his time; no one was able to listen to him above the ear-splitting two-tone siren of the fire alarm.

'Lifeboat stations. Lifeboat stations.'

The two men rushed down two more flights of steps to the engine room, which the last of the engineers were just abandoning.

'Get back to your posts!' Olberg ordered.

'No way!' his chief engineer retorted as he pushed past. 'Take a look in there and you'll see what I mean!'

147

The explosion had blown Tammy right off her feet. One minute she was standing in the casino, enjoying her champagne cocktail. Next instant she found herself slammed into the far wall with shocking force as the world went haywire.

'A bomb!' someone yelled. 'Has to be a bomb.' Tammy felt her heart begin to pound uncontrollably as she tasted the prospect of imminent death for the first time in her life.

'Get out onto the decks!' the casino manager yelled. 'Into the lifeboats!'

There was a rush for the exit. Tammy was about to follow. Then she saw the strongroom door. It was still open.

The safe clearly visible inside.

With the keys still in the lock.

148

Gwen and Tehpoe made it to the fringes of the forest.

'We can't take a trail,' Gwen told Tehpoe. 'That's the first thing they'll think of. We have to go our own way.'

They started to push through the vegetation, using all their strength to force a route. The tendrils of a hundred different tropical plants snagged at their hands, their legs, their feet.

But Gwen kept on shouldering a route through, her teeth gritted with determination, her hand clamped firmly to Tehpoe's hand as she pulled him along.

The mobile flashed back into her mind. She waited until they were sufficiently distant from the camp and pulled the unit out. Now was the moment to make a fast call.

She dialled her sister's number.

149

Olberg and the first officer entered the engine room; what they saw there was something they could never have imagined in their most vivid nightmares.

Two of the engines had smoke pouring out of them. The machines were still operating at full power, the turbos screaming as they pumped out thousands of horsepower to the twin screws which propelled the ship.

And there was worse: the furnace-like heat of the blaze on the other side of the metal bulkhead was having an extraordinary effect; it was actually *melting* the steel wall which was the engine room's last barrier of protection.

Then the welds blew. As Olberg and his officer watched, transfixed with horror, the engine room began to flood with burning kerosene.

150

Todd was still holding on to the root, and supporting Isabella at the same time, but he was fast approaching the point where his strength would fail. The girl was also getting weaker and weaker. Once or twice she had almost slipped down the muddy slope into the pool.

His arms were gripped by the most excruciating cramps; Todd had no idea how much more he could take. The pathetic little ledge he was using as a foothold was barely enough to take his weight.

'Don't give up!' he told Isabella as he shook her gently. 'We have to hold on.'

Todd knew that he could not support her if she fell unconscious. And beneath them the piranhas were still circling.

151

The four gas turbine generators were delivering pretty much their full 52,400 horsepower load as the burning kerosene engulfed them.

Engine number one died immediately, the cabling controlling its internal control systems melting in the extreme heat and causing an automatic shut down. Engine number two was more problematic. The turbine, already running red hot, began to shudder as blades began to melt one by one.

The engine didn't shut down so that the turbine could gradually lose its momentum. It seized in a split second. Thirteen thousand horsepower had, for a moment or two, nowhere to go as the main drive shafts locked.

Then the thirty tonne engine twisted off its mountings and punched with extraordinary force through the hull of the ship. The hole was big enough to drive a truck through.

And it was letting in one hundred and ninety thousand gallons of sea water a second.

The *Cayman Glory* was going down.

152

Ella ran to the nearest lifeboat station. There were thirty or forty passengers mustered nearby, frantically trying to scramble into their lifejackets. A news helicopter buzzed in overhead, a cameraman hanging out of the open door.

'Lifeboat stations. Lifeboat stations.' The siren was blasting off every second or two.

Suddenly Ella heard the shrill tone of her mobile. She saw immediately the call was from Liberia.

'Gwen?'

'I have to make this fast, Ella, the mission was attacked, we're in desperate trouble, I need to you to contact . . . '

At that instant the vessel was struck another grievous blow from an explosion deep in the superstructure.

Ella was blown off her feet. As she crashed to the deck, the mobile slipped out of her hands and fell overboard.

153

'What are we going to do with him?' Fran asked.

'We can't leave him here,' Hicks snapped. 'Let's get him to hospital at least.'

Fran gave her husband a grateful look. He was a bluff old character sometimes but he always made the right decision when the chips were down.

'Take us to the nearest hospital,' Hicks told the chauffeur.

'They are closed. By military orders.' The poor man was now sweating with fear.

'All right. We'll take him back to the hotel.' The two men began to manoeuvre the young monk into the back seat of the vehicle.

As they pulled away, Hicks glanced back through the rear window; two of the troop carriers were hot on their tail. 'They're following us, aren't they?' Fran said, her voice loaded with dread.

154

Murray West had returned to his cabin in his wheelchair after his successful heist on the old lady. Now he was wondering what the hell to do as choking smoke trickled in through the ceiling vent.

He could hear stewards shouting in the corridor outside: 'Make your way to the lifeboat stations. Do not try and use the lifts. We repeat, do not try and use the lifts.'

Do not use the lifts? He was eight decks down—deep in the lowest depths of the vessel.

Murray's disability made it impossible for him to climb stairs. If he couldn't use the lifts he was as good as dead.

Murray thought about his mobile. He could call Tammy. Tammy would help him. *Surely she would help him?* He pressed the call button and waited anxiously for the ringing tone which would confirm he'd got through.

If ever he needed her, it was now.

155

Thiago was enjoying his drink in Porto Velho when a breaking news story came up on the TV screen.

Images of a sinking cruise ship on fire in Sydney harbour. The footage came from a helicopter and was intensely dramatic, the cameraman zooming in to pick out individual passengers as they fought to clamber into lifeboats.

'Give me a Brahma,' Thiago told the barman. Moments later he had the ice cold beer in his hand.

The television images showed small boats arriving on the scene in Sydney. Thiago couldn't tear his eyes away and, along with the rest of the bar, he let out a cheer as a woman and child were pulled into a lifeboat.

The images provoked a strong pang of guilt in the smuggler.

Had he done the right thing to ignore those screams out on the river? The cries were haunting him even now.

156

Tammy felt the mobile vibrating against her thigh. Instantly she knew who it would be. Murray's number on the screen.

'Tammy?' She could hear the panic in his voice. 'I'm down on level eight. Outside my cabin. I can't get out, there's no one to help me.'

'Oh God, Murray . . . '

Tammy stalled. She knew full well that Murray would not be able to get out without assistance. But if she went down to try and rescue her lover she would be throwing away the opportunity of a lifetime with that safe full of money.

'Murray, I'm trapped on one of the upper decks,' she lied, 'I can't get down to you. They won't let me go back down the stairs.'

There was a stunned silence from the other end of the line. 'I gotta go, Murray. Good luck.'

And with that she terminated the call.

157

Hannah and the cop had been at the clinic having their burns dressed. Now they were back in the rescue helicopter and heading for police headquarters where Hannah would be booked and charged.

But just minutes before touching down at Sydney's central heliport the pilot got a call.

From their vantage point two thousand feet above the city they had already seen the smoke rising from the *Cayman Glory* and there had been some intensive radio traffic coming into the cockpit.

'We have to divert. There's no time to put you two down,' the winchman told Hannah. 'You guys are going to be on board for a little longer.'

Hannah watched through the port-side window as the helicopter flew over the Harbour Bridge, heading for the looming profile of the burning ship.

She was beginning to realize they were flying right into the heart of a truly monumental disaster.

158

Gwen and Tehpoe were crashing as fast as they could through the trackless jungle. The skin of their arms had been flayed by 'stay-a-while' thorns but every step of progress was giving them more hope.

The call had been a disaster. Cut off after just a few seconds for reasons that Gwen could not fathom. But she hoped her sister had heard enough to alert the charity headquarters at least.

But then came the sound that Gwen had most feared.

The savage sound of barking coming from behind them. And, fainter, the cries of the rebels as they followed on. The dogs *had* woken Kickback and his men.

There was no sense in running now. The dogs were too fast for that. Gwen pulled Tehpoe into a thicket of the densest vegetation they could find.

Gwen held Tehpoe close, wanting to protect him. She could feel his heart pulsing beneath her palm, so fast it was more a vibration than a series of single beats.

159

**DECK EIGHT, THE *CAYMAN GLORY*,
SYDNEY, AUSTRALIA**

Captain Stian Olberg quit the engine room and arrived at passenger deck eight. The corridor was filled with smoke, illuminated by the feeble emergency lights, and he wanted to be sure no one had been left behind.

'Hey! Anybody here?' he called.

A cough. A man's cough. There *was* someone there.

Olberg kept himself low to the floor—a handkerchief held to his mouth as he cautiously edged forward. Towards the end of the corridor he found a male passenger next to an overturned wheelchair; the man was weak but he was still alive.

Olberg recognized the guy's face—realized the passenger was the disabled man he had welcomed onto the ship just hours before.

'Get onto my back,' Olberg ordered him. The captain crouched down on the floor and waited as Murray managed with some difficulty to clasp his hands around his neck.

He staggered to his feet and headed for the stairs.

160

Tammy had the keys in her hands. That piercing alarm was still raging *'Lifeboat stations, lifeboat stations.'* The casino had been evacuated; she was on her own.

Staring at the safe.

At that precise moment there were two largely conflicting desires raging inside this career criminal: firstly the internal voice that was screaming, 'GET OFF THE SINKING SHIP,' and then a second one which was almost as loud: 'THERE IS A MILLION DOLLARS HERE FOR THE TAKING.'

Tammy turned the key, heaved on the metal door of the safe. The bundles of cash were sitting obediently on the shelves, beautiful, tightly bound angels of deliverance from a life of poverty and strife. Dozens of them.

It was the best thing Tammy had ever seen in her life.

161

THE COSMOS HOTEL, YANGON, MYANMAR

Wai Yan had regained consciousness during the short journey to the hotel.

Now, Hicks took the young monk in his arms, a movement which caused the boy's broken leg to twist. He uttered a cry of pain as the Australian tourist headed for the revolving doors of the hotel only to find that the hotel manager and his head of security were blocking the way.

'I am very sorry,' the manager told Hicks. 'I cannot have this boy in the hotel.'

'He's injured,' Hicks barked, his patience tested to the limit, 'and the hospitals are closed. So what else do you suggest? That I leave him in the street?'

The manager saw the troop carriers heading for the hotel. He swore beneath his breath.

'I want to speak to the Australian Ambassador,' Hicks continued emphatically. 'Get me the phone number. Now I'm taking him to my room and I want you to call a doctor for him.'

162

Olberg stumbled up the step and reached deck six. He was winded and disorientated in the thick smoke, and the majority of passengers had now evacuated the stairwell so that he felt very much alone with this disabled passenger clinging desperately to his back . . .

He was dripping with sweat. The stairwell was tilted at an awkward angle as the boat continued to sink—so much so now that he was having to haul himself bodily upwards using the handrail for support.

'Leave me,' Murray told the captain. 'We won't make it. At least give yourself a chance.'

A new blast of smoke and fumes erupted from the decks below. Olberg realized that the floors beneath them were now burning out of control.

The sprinkler system had failed.

'We keep going.' Olberg started to climb the steps once more.

163
THE COSMOS HOTEL, YANGON, MYANMAR, ASIA

As soon as they reached their hotel room, John Hicks placed the young monk on the bed and immediately crossed to the window. Eight floors below he could see more military vehicles pulling up to join the two troop carriers which were already out front. Then, right at the end of the street, they saw a line of tanks rumbling in the direction of the hotel.

From the other end of the street came a wave of protestors, more than before, with perhaps three or four hundred monks in the crowd.

'It's spiralling out of control,' he said. Hicks sat down heavily on a chair. He suddenly looked very pale. And he was breathing hard.

'John? John, are you sure you're all right?' Fran asked him.

Her husband clutched at his chest for a few seconds as if a spasm of pain was pulsing there. Then he forced a smile at his wife and managed—somewhat shakily—to stand.

'Nonsense,' he said, 'I'm as fit as a fiddle.'

164

Ella pressed the 'launch' button. The lifeboat was descending, swinging just out of reach. She realized she would have to jump for it.

'I'll catch you!' the crewman called. She gave a great leap.

The crewman held out his hands to help Ella on board but the wounds on her hands had opened up in the violence of the last explosion and they were now slippery with blood. Ella fumbled against his fingers as she tried to get a grip.

Too late.

Ella fell, crashing into the water. For a few moments she was underneath the waves then, as she bobbed back up, the lifeboat engine kicked into life and the craft was pulling away. 'Hey! Here!' Ella cried out with all her strength.

But no one was listening. The lifeboat was powering away from her.

165

Hannah was staring in horror out of the open door of the rescue helicopter as it manoeuvred into position above the *Cayman Glory*. It was a grandstand view of the scene, a catastrophe happening in real time right in front of her eyes.

The vessel was listing hard to starboard, with vast quantities of jet black smoke billowing from the back of the ship.

The sea was covered with an oily sheen, the air thick with so much black smoke that she could see little more than a hundred metres in any direction. Small boats—fishing vessels, tourist cruisers—had rushed to the rescue and they only added to the chaos of the scene as they buzzed to and fro, trying to pull survivors from the sea.

'Get back in your seat,' the winchman told her.

He started to prepare his rescue gear.

166

Marko and Paul Masters reached the sinking hulk of the *Cayman Glory* as a third explosion rent the air.

'Help!' a man called to them from the midst of the floating debris.

Masters turned the inflatable towards him. For a moment Marko lost sight of the survivor. Then he resurfaced.

'There!' The man was choking, half drowned, his hair slick with fuel oil, his eyes wide with disbelief at this living nightmare. The Zodiac pulled up alongside him and Marko grabbed the man by the hands.

'Marko?' the man gasped in astonishment. 'Is that you?'

Marko stared in confusion at the man. For a few moments, lost in the stress of the moment, and confused by the slick of oil covering the victim's head, he had absolutely no idea who it was.

Then he clicked: 'Bruce? No way!'

167

Thiago decided to get back out on the river. The rescue footage from the sinking ship had inspired him to check out those cries again.

It was the sight of children being pulled out of the sea that had done it.

He paid up for his drinks and hurried through the streets of Porto Velho. At the landing stage he untied his canoe and pushed out into the river.

The current was exceptionally strong; the rain had really boosted the flow of the Jari and Thiago knew he could easily overturn in the rapids if he wasn't careful.

He steered a cautious route upriver, still wary that he was stepping right into a police trap.

Then he saw a light. Very faint. But a light nonetheless. Beneath the trees next to the bank just downstream from the rapids. Exactly where he had heard those voices before.

168

Tammy had found a suitcase in the casino office. Now she jammed in the last brick of dollar bills and let out a big breath of satisfaction. The case was overloaded, bulging at the seams; she had to sit on it and pinch the top and bottom together to close the reluctant zip.

'Lifeboat stations. Lifeboat stations.'

She was satisfied with her work.

A fortune. Well over a million. Perhaps even two.

Now all she had to do was get the heck off the sinking ship.

Had she left it too late? Tammy knew she had pushed her luck further than she ever had before.

Out onto the casino floor. The suitcase was heavier than she had anticipated. She slipped on a slick vein of oil which had dripped from the ceiling. Slammed on her side with a painful thud. Got back up, gritted her teeth.

Tammy saw the exit through the haze of smoke; just twenty metres away.

169

The shock of seeing his buddy gave Marko a weird twist in his gut. How many years was it since they had seen each other . . . ? Why was this happening now? It totally freaked him out.

Marko hauled his friend onto the inflatable where he collapsed in a heap.

'You're OK, buddy,' Marko told him. He handed Bruce a plastic bottle of fresh water and watched as he washed oil out of his mouth and spat over the side.

Then Bruce collapsed on the floor of the inflatable.

'There's another survivor! Over there!' Masters yelled from the back.

The Zodiac turned back towards the burning ship.

170

The two tracker dogs found Tehpoc and Gwen cowering in the thick vegetation. The savage creatures flushed them out of the hiding place and they ran for their lives, pushing blindly through the clinging creepers and hanging vines as the rebels closed in.

'Stop them!' The guttural bark of Commander Kickback rang out from behind them. The percussive crack of an automatic weapon rattled the thick tropical air as dirt kicked up.

Tehpoe was struggling. His illness had weakened him and he was tiring fast. Gwen picked him up, holding him in her arms as she ran down the single file track through the jungle.

Then she tripped on a root. Fell to the ground in a heap with Tehpoe sprawled on top of her. Her satellite phone fell from her pocket, tumbled into the dirt.

'On my back!' she told Tehpoe as she regained her feet. But the guards were closing in.

171

Tammy pushed the door open and fell out onto the upper recreation deck of the *Cayman Glory*.

At first she could see little through the smoke but then she got lucky and a rescue helicopter spotted her. It flew over to her position, the pilot putting the machine into a hovering position some ten metres or so above the deck. It was a perilous stance; smoke and flames were licking frighteningly close to the skids.

Then a steel cable was snaking down towards the deck, a basket like a cradle on the end.

'Climb in,' a voice yelled through a megaphone. 'And hang on to the safety lines.' Tammy grabbed the case and tried to haul it up into the basket.

'Ditch the case,' the voice screamed down on the megaphone. 'Ditch the suitcase and get into the basket immediately.'

'No!' she screamed up. 'I can't leave it!'

172

Captain Olberg staggered out onto the upper deck, Murray still on his back. He saw an open life jacket store—with one of the distinctive jackets clearly visible inside.

One life jacket. One chance of salvation.

He could have taken that jacket for himself. He could have walked away from the semi-conscious disabled man at his feet, got himself into the sea where there was a fighting chance of safety.

But Captain Stian Olberg wasn't a man to think of himself when there were others to be saved.

He retrieved the life jacket then bent down and began to thread Murray's arms through the straps. Murray felt the life jacket tighten around his chest as the air filled it.

Then Olberg began to drag his passenger across the deck.

173

Thiago steered cautiously towards the strange light.

'Please! Help us!' Now Thiago could hear the voice of the young girl.

Then came a splashing noise, followed by the most piercing screams he had ever heard in his life.

'OK,' he called, 'I'm coming now!'

Thiago felt the nose of the canoe nudge against the over-hanging trees of the riverbank. It was a desperate vision; in the water up to his waist was a gringo with fair hair. He was holding a young girl in his arms, trying with all his strength to keep her out of the water as she screamed in abject terror.

The river water was bright red, and boiling with activity around the gringo and for a second or two Thiago thought he was being attacked by caymans.

Then, with a sickening lurch in his stomach, he realized that it was a school of piranhas.

174

THE *CAYMAN GLORY*, SYDNEY, AUSTRALIA

The *Cayman Glory* was two thirds filled with sea water and listing at twenty-five degrees.

For the moment she was still—just—afloat, but the fire had now consumed the theatre, the crew quarters, and five of the eleven restaurants, and the atrium had been reduced to a chaos of twisted metal and waterfalls of melted glass.

More importantly, at least for the imminent status of the vessel, the vast heat had caused the central bulkhead to fracture in its entirety. The whole wall was melted away above the water line. The structural integrity of the *Cayman Glory* was fatally compromised.

The marine grade metal skin of the ship was all that was holding her together. And with every wave smashing into her hull the welds were splitting and fracturing.

With a banshee shriek of tortured metal the eighty-five thousand tonne vessel began to break her own back; the forward and aft sections of keel separating as the midsection of the ship rose high into the air.

THE HICKSES' HOTEL SUITE, COSMOS HOTEL, YANGON, MYANMAR

The bellboy rapped hard on the door of the Hickses' suite. Hicks checked the security porthole mirror and opened the door.

'Fax for you, sir.'

Hicks opened the envelope and studied the fax; his brow creasing as he tried to comprehend what he was reading.

The Cayman Glory *was sinking after a series of explosions on board. She was going down in two hundred fathoms of water just outside Sydney Harbour. Many lives had already been lost and more were expected.*

Sinking? Lives lost? John Hicks felt immediately sick as he read the fax again. The *Cayman Glory* was his last and most successful throw of the dice as a businessman and now she was disappearing beneath the waves for . . . for what reason? Terrorist attack? Some random fire on board?

And people had been killed. It was too terrible to contemplate.

Tammy got both hands on the suitcase of cash, biting her lip with the effort as she finally humped it into the rescue basket. She held the steel cables and tried to get in on top of it. But the case had filled the space to the brim and she was left clinging on to the edges.

'Ditch the case!' The winchman's shouts were increasingly stressed as he saw Tammy trying, and failing, to climb into the basket.

The winch cable began to swipe from side to side as the helicopter rocked in the sky. The case gave the basket momentum and Tammy was slammed against the steel bulkhead of the deck.

She was winded. She fell away from the basket.

'We can't stay here!' the winchman screamed down. 'Find a life jacket! Try and get into the water!'

The helicopter banked away towards the back of the ship, the case still nestled in the rescue basket.

177

Gwen was running as fast as she could but she was slowed by Tehpoe's weight on her back and a few seconds later the rebel guards were on them.

Gwen and Tehpoe were dragged through the dirt of the jungle floor and brought before the commander. One of his men had noticed the satphone where it had dropped onto the ground and he gave it to his master. Kickback now examined it closely before snapping savagely at Gwen.

'You have tested my patience,' the commander raged. 'And now I am at my limit.'

He nodded to one of his men. Gwen and Tehpoe had their arms tied behind their backs.

'We will go back to the camp,' Kickback continued, 'and in the meantime I will have a think about what punishment you both deserve.'

The two escapees were surrounded by the rebel troops and Captain Kickback led the way back through the forest, the hungry dogs still snapping at Gwen's and Tehpoe's heels.

178

To Captain Stian Olberg, the sound of the helicopter blades chopping through the air above them was the sound of salvation.

The helicopter shifted position, the pilot adjusting so that the rescue basket came flapping against the deck on its steel cable. Olberg and Murray stared at the suitcase, wondering what on earth they were supposed to do with it.

'Get the case out of the basket!' the winchman ordered through his megaphone.

Murray and the captain grabbed hold of the suitcase but it was snagged in the netting of the basket and they were struggling to shift it.

An explosion rent the air, sending a new plume of black smoke up towards the helicopter.

'All right!' the winchman screamed. 'Climb on top of it, but one only! We don't have the fuel to carry more weight.'

179

The crowd of monks was becoming agitated and vocal as General Pauk Taw pulled up in his command vehicle. A few small stones had been thrown at the government troops who were milling around outside the hotel and they had retaliated with a baton charge.

General Pauk Taw climbed onto a tank. He paused for effect for a few moments, staring out into the crowd of monks with an icy stare which was pure arrogance. Not a single man or child out there dared to meet his gaze.

'So! One of your number—a criminal on the run from the authorities—has been taken into the protection of foreign spies here in this hotel. I am going to arrest this collaborator right away. Then he will be punished as is right and proper under the laws of this country!'

The general jumped down from the tank and handed the megaphone to an aide. Then he beckoned to six of his most trusted officers—brutal looking men who would not hesitate to carry out his every command.

He barked an order. They drew their pistols. Then they followed General Pauk Taw into the lobby of the hotel.

Olberg knew he had to lift Murray into the basket, wedge him on top of the stuck suitcase.

'Get in!' He picked up Murray with a monumental show of strength and lifted him into the rescue basket.

The disabled man sat on top of the suitcase and clutched the safety lines as he was winched up towards the helicopter. Seconds later the aircraft peeled away across the ocean, heading back for Sydney.

Olberg moved immediately to the edge of the deck and stared out into the abyss. There was no sign of any rescue craft, just burning bunker oil and roiling smoke as the ship went down.

He saw a net stretching down to the water.

It was the same cargo net that had hauled the lobsters onto the back of the boat. The one that Bruce had got snagged.

Olberg began to climb down it.

181

'Swim towards me!' Thiago called, but the gringo was losing blood fast and he seemed incapable of answering as he sank further down into the river.

He was still valiantly holding the girl out of the water, and at a terrible cost to himself.

Thiago urged the boat closer—deeper into the pool. He grabbed hold of the girl and pulled her onto the canoe where she collapsed in a sobbing heap. He could see plenty of bite marks but it looked as if she would survive.

'Save him, please!' she gasped.

Thiago turned back for the gringo but he was too late. The heroic traveller had already disappeared beneath the surface of the river and all that was left was a patch of red water and a boiling mass of predators writhing in the depths.

The piranhas had won their prize.

182

Tammy watched the rescue helicopter peel away from the ship, the figure of a rescued passenger suspended beneath it. There was something that looked familiar about the silhouette of the man who had been saved but she couldn't be sure.

It was a moment of supreme loneliness and despair.

She had gambled everything on that one big heist and now she was paying the price of failure.

The steel floor beneath her feet began to flex and crack. An instant later, with a shriek of rendering metal, the entire deck ripped open and Tammy was thrown into the gaping hole within.

She landed in the chaotic space that just a short time before had been the well ordered environment of the casino. Her fall ended on the green baize surface of a roulette table.

Tammy was staring at the wheel of chance as the sea water filled her lungs.

183

Captain Stian Olberg clambered down the cargo net until he was level with the water. Then he collapsed into the sea. He had inhaled so much carbon monoxide that his blood oxygen levels were critically low.

He managed to re-surface but he knew he was too weak and disorientated to swim. Then an object appeared in front of him.

It was the Zodiac piloted by Paul Masters.

Marko leaned out. 'Take hold of my hand!' he yelled to the man.

But the captain was too heavy and he seemed to be snagged on something.

'He's tangled up in some debris,' Masters shouted, pointing beneath the waves.

Marko looked over the side and saw the problem. Some netting had snagged the man's legs, tangling him up in a cat's cradle of filaments.

Marko grabbed a knife from Masters and dived into the turbulent sea.

184

Fran called from inside the room: 'Is everything all right, John?'

Hicks clutched at his chest as a sudden crushing wave of pain hit him. He staggered to the balcony, reaching out to grasp it as he bent over in agony.

'Are you OK, sir?' the bellboy asked, uncertain what to do. Hicks inhaled heavily as a second agonizing spasm rippled across his chest. The stress of the day had culminated in this disastrous news and his heart couldn't take it.

'Get my . . . wife . . . ' he gasped, but the words were too quiet for the boy to understand.

Hicks felt his vision narrowing, blackness engulfing him as he felt his heart ready to explode.

Then he died: his overworked, diseased heart giving up the fight in a final giant tremor. The boy lunged forward but he couldn't catch the Australian in time.

Hicks toppled over the balcony and fell towards the floor of the atrium eight storeys below.

185

Captain Kickback led his ragtag convoy of men into the camp. Their two prisoners were thrown to the floor in the centre of the parade ground.

'Remove their ties,' Kickback screamed. The rebels did as they were asked and Tehpoe and Gwen scrambled awkwardly to their feet, rubbing their sore wrists to get circulation back in their hands.

'Get me a blade!' Kickback ordered one of his men.

The man wandered drunkenly to a shack and returned with a machete in his hands.

He handed the weapon to the commander who stared at Gwen with the most terrible expression of evil.

'Oh no,' Gwen whispered, 'please, God, no . . .'

Commander Kickback gave the machete to Tehpoe.

'Now is your moment,' the rebel leader told him, 'to show us all what you are made of, boy.'

186

Ella felt her legs dragged down by an almost irresistible force. As a former sea captain herself she knew what this was—the ship, as it sank, was displacing millions of gallons of sea water, dragging it down, creating a whirlpool effect at the surface which could suck down small boats with ease.

Then. And then. She saw something floating nearby. *Floating*. If she could only grab hold of that blue painted object—whatever it was—Ella knew she might yet be saved.

She swam forward a few straggly strokes. Her lungs were like crumpled crisp packets, virtually collapsed under the force of invasive sea water.

She grabbed hold of the floating object. Salvation. It could support her weight with ease.

Then, with a shock of realization which cut to the core of her being, she saw what the object was.

It was the resin figurine of the Virgin Mary.

187

RIO JARI, AMAZON BASIN, BRAZIL

Thiago steered his canoe towards the main jetty at Porto
Velho. There was a charitable medical mission in town and
he knew they would treat the young girl free of charge.

'Get her to the clinic will you?' he asked the night watchman. 'She's been attacked by piranhas.' The watchman knew
Thiago of old, and the ten dollar note he was offering would
come in handy.

Before she was taken away, the girl spoke urgently to
him: 'My mother is dying,' she told him. 'We live in the first
cabin on the right by the tributary of the Rio Elva. Can you
go to her, bring her back here to the hospital?'

Thiago looked into the pleading eyes of the young girl.
His own wife had gone through a difficult labour on her
own some years before so he instinctively felt sympathy for
the girl's mother.

'I will try my best,' he promised.

Moments later he was heading upriver for the rapids, a
black shadow melting into the dark night.

188

Marko forced himself beneath the waves. Visibility was extremely limited—perhaps a metre of murky vision at best.

The situation was worse than he had anticipated.

The captain was well and truly entangled in the net. Marko ran his fingers along the nylon, sensing that it was strong, that cutting it would be a battle.

He slashed with the knife.

He had to surface frequently for breath, each time feeling weaker and more exhausted.

'I can't stay here much longer!' Masters called out to Marko.

Marko forced himself down one more time. He sliced through the final section of the mesh.

The man was free.

189
THE COSMOS HOTEL, YANGON, MYANMAR

John Hicks's body fell eight storeys down into the atrium of the hotel in less than one point five seconds. The fall was utterly silent, witnessed by nobody except for the horrified bellboy who had delivered the fateful fax.

The falling corpse hit General Pauk Taw as he crossed the atrium of the hotel with his entourage of thugs. The impact was instantly fatal, the one hundred and ten kilo body of the Australian businessman hitting the hard-line chief of Myanmar's Defence Service full on the head, breaking two of the vertebrae in his neck and crushing his windpipe.

The general fell stone dead to the marble floor, his arms entwined in a curious and macabre embrace with the body of the Australian.

The general's bodyguard were stunned into silence. They stared at the two corpses as the fax gently fluttered down, finally landing on Hicks's face where it sat like a shroud.

190

Marko grabbed a lungful of air as he saw Masters pull the captain on board the Zodiac. Then he felt a tugging on his legs.

The netting had snagged him as it had done the captain.

He felt the weight of it dragging him down. With every passing moment he was having to work harder to stay afloat. He was treading water as aggressively as he could—and trying to get to the Zodiac—but he was still getting pulled under the surface.

Then—with a tremor of fear enough to make him want to cry out loud—he realized what was happening. The net was still attached to the guard rail at the stern of the *Cayman Glory*.

The ship was going down.

And he was going with it.

191

The rebel soldiers dragged Gwen to the bloodstained chopping block. Her tunic was pulled up to expose her left arm.

'This woman has tried to escape with my favourite new recruit,' the commander cried. 'So now she will lose her arm. That will tell the world that we are serious.'

The commander's men started to chant, some shooting off pistol shots into the air. Tehpoe felt sickness rising inside him as he turned the machete nervously in his hands.

'Now prove that you are a warrior and a man,' the commander said gently to Tehpoe. 'Strike off her arm with a single blow. It is time for this woman to understand that her god has forsaken her.'

'My God will never forsake me,' Gwen replied with as much dignity as she could muster.

At this, the commander laughed.

'My dear lady,' he said, 'you are about to discover that there *is* no God!'

Marko redoubled his efforts to get free. He hacked furiously at the mesh, but the knife had become blunt. The Zodiac was swept ever further from him as the waves crashed crazily into the inflatable.

The smoke thickened as the *Cayman Glory* went into its death throes. Fire raged everywhere—even on the sea. Next time Marko came up for air the Zodiac was no longer visible. To escape the raging fire, Masters had had to pull away from the side of the vessel.

Marko was on his own.

He made one last monumental effort, twisting his body violently to try and free himself from the net.

But the filaments had his lower body firmly gripped.

Ella was still holding on to the resin figurine of the Virgin Mary as the inflatable boat pulled up alongside her. The *Cayman Glory* had almost vanished beneath the waves and the smoke was now being blown away from the scene.

Paul Masters had to use force to prise her fingers off the figurine to get her onto the Zodiac. The statuette floated away, bobbing up and down in the waves until it was lost to view as the Zodiac headed back towards the harbour.

Ella slumped onto the wet floor of the inflatable, trembling with a mixture of shock and relief, trying to make sense of all that had happened.

Then she snapped out of it. Remembered that desperate garbled message from Gwen. The mission had been attacked. She *had* to call Gwen.

'You have a mobile?' Ella asked the man at the helm of the inflatable. 'I need to make a call right now.'

CENTRAL HOSPITAL, SYDNEY, AUSTRALIA

The rescue helicopter came in to land at the heliport at Sydney's central hospital. From her position next to the winchman, Hannah could see an army of medics, TV crews and other emergency personnel waiting for the victims.

As soon as the skids hit the deck they were evacuating the worst injured, including the disabled guy Murray. Hannah and the cop refused offers of help.

The emergency team quickly disappeared into the casualty ward. The heli crew had gone in with them leaving just the pilot to power down the engines.

'You still going to arrest me?' Hannah asked the cop.

The guy thought about it for a few moments; then his expression mellowed out.

'I think not . . . Maybe what we just saw has put a new perspective on it.'

'OK. Thank you.'

'So long,' said the cop, holding out his hand. 'See you around.'

Hannah shook his hand. 'Yeah. Maybe we'll go on another bike ride together some time.'

The cop gave a grim smile, then he walked away to the hospital entrance to assist the medics. He was a good guy at heart, she thought.

195

Masters handed Ella his mobile. She was so stricken by her ordeal that she could only just get her frozen fingers to operate the tiny buttons.

Moments later the international ring tone sounded loud and clear. Ella heard the click of the connection. She knew she would have to scream to make herself heard above the noise of the outboard.

'Gwen?'

A man's voice replied; he sounded drunk, or drugged.

'Hello? Who is this? I was just telling your Australian friend that there is no God.'

Ella could hardly hear above the roar of the engine, the crashing of the waves. She pressed the mobile harder against her ear. Salt water spray was crashing against her body.

'Gwen?'

She felt a wave of elemental emotion engulf her; her miraculous salvation seemed an answer to a question she had been asking all her life.

'There is a God,' she shouted, 'there *is* a God!'

196

General Pauk Taw was dead. Word of the bizarre tragedy inside the hotel had spread quickly through the waiting militia, and also through the crowd of waiting protestors.

The crowd was shocked but also energized by the news, for the demise of the hard-line general might open the door for a more moderate future.

The body was loaded into a military ambulance and driven away.

One of the senior monks approached the hotel entrance where the general's men still stood guard.

'Sir,' the monk addressed the lieutenant with his hands pressed together in a gesture of prayer, 'one of our brothers has been injured and he is inside the hotel. We wish to take him to a hospital.'

The lieutenant hesitated, unsure of what he should do. 'Please,' continued the monk, 'let us pass.'

It was a pivotal moment, and the lieutenant was vividly aware that his actions would dictate the mood of the city over the following hours or even days.

He looked to his men and he could see in their faces that they would accept his decision if he stood them down.

He motioned to his men to stand aside.

Myanmar's Saffron Revolution had taken its first great step.

197

'What is this?' the commander screamed at the phone. 'What is this sorcery?' The call had come right at the crucial moment, just as Tehpoe was about to make the blow.

The commander placed the mobile to his ear once more and again heard the woman saying the words:

'There is a God.'

He clicked on the mobile then threw it to the ground. He unshouldered his Kalashnikov and fired bullets at the satellite phone until it was shattered into nothing more than splinters of plastic and fragments of circuit boards.

He looked around his men, swaying unsteadily on his feet. He vomited red liquid onto the ground, retching long and hard as his stomach emptied.

'There is a God,' he whispered to his troops. 'Do none of you have anything to say to that?' Then an overwhelming weariness seemed to come over him.

He began to weep.

And once he began to cry, Commander Kickback could not find it in himself to stop.

198
CENTRAL HOSPITAL, SYDNEY, AUSTRALIA

Hannah was about to step from the helicopter but at that moment something happened that was bizarre enough to leave her frozen in her seat: she recognized one of the doctors milling around the chopper. For a beat or two she could not place the tall blond man. Then she had it.

It was the guy whose motorbike she had stolen that morning. And in that instant his eyes met hers and the connection was made between them.

'I know you,' he said uncertainly. 'From somewhere . . .'

Then he got it. She could see it in his eyes. He knew exactly who she was and the effect was as if he'd just taken a bullet. Every millilitre of blood drained out of his face as he struggled to piece this thing together.

'You stole my bike . . . but . . . how . . . why are you here? Just a coincidence or what?'

Hannah could not answer. She *had* no answer.

One of the other medics called for help and the doctor was forced to leave.

The look he gave Hannah as he walked away was one she would never forget. Her presence had shaken him to the core.

199

The lobsters were stored in a huge cold room situated at the aft end of one of the *Cayman Glory*'s galleys.

The cool room was constructed of layered aluminium with a foam heat trap built in. It was no match for the extraordinary forces at work as the *Cayman Glory* broke her back. The cool room imploded as the metal doors pinged off their hinges.

Two thousand, eight hundred, and eighty live Maine lobsters spilled from the cartons as the ship went down.

They tumbled down to the sea bed where they found that the water was warmer than the cool New England currents they were used to. Lobsters are hardy and adaptable creatures though, and at least now they had a fighting chance.

And, with scores of dead millionaires lying on the sea bed there would certainly be plenty of food available.

Rather like the first class passengers of the *Cayman Glory*, lobsters do like their food to be fresh.

200
CENTRAL HOSPITAL, SYDNEY, AUSTRALIA

Hannah quit the helicopter and found herself alone. Then her sharp eyes picked something up: there was a suitcase stuck in the rescue basket which had been dangling beneath the chopper.

Sticking out of the zip she could see bundles of hundred dollar bills. She quickly pulled the suitcase free from the rescue basket.

It was heavy, she noticed, really very heavy indeed.

This was something she *had* to check out.

Hannah carried the bag across to the hospital building. She put on a look of bored nonchalance, as if she walked across a heliport every day of her life with a bulging suitcase in her hands.

She went to the ladies' room and locked the door. Then she sprung the catches on the case.

Three minutes later, Hannah Williams walked out of the emergency room with the suitcase in her hands. No one tried to stop her. No one even noticed that she was leaving. Out in the street she hailed a cab.

'Take me to the railway station please,' she commanded the driver. As always, she wished her brother Todd was with her, just to share the moment . . .

'I'm going to Brisbane.'

201

The tears coursed down Commander Kickback's cheeks in a cascade of misery which was greater than he could ever have imagined.

And still his men were silent.

Gwen stared at Tehpoe, willing him not to say anything.

Commander Kickback took off his mirror RayBans and rubbed his raw red eyes. He sat heavily on the tree stump which had seen so much innocent slaughter, heedless of the blood which now seeped into his combat fatigues. An air of great sadness overcame him, a sadness as wide and deep and impenetrable as the jungle that surrounded him.

'There is a God,' he whispered.

'There is a GOD!' This time a manic scream. His men looked at each other in terror—they had seen some crazy mood swings by their unpredictable leader but this one was something completely new.

Finally he gestured at Gwen.

'Release her,' he said quietly.

Then he addressed Tehpoe.

'And you, boy. I think it is time for you to go home.'

297

Marko knew with a dread surge of terror that the struggle was over. He could feel his lungs heavy with sea water and his efforts to break free from the netting had achieved nothing.

The smoke was thicker than ever, enveloping him in a blanket of black fog through which the occasional cry of drowning terror would distantly echo. The sinking ship was invisible to him but he could hear the deep groaning and cracking of splintering metal as it sank.

He was in pain. His lungs burned as salt water raged like acid on delicate tissue. He wanted to close his eyes, to slip quietly beneath the waves.

Then something emerged from the clouds of smoke. A ragged, winged creature: an Australian Painted Lady on the final flight of its life.

Marko reached up with his hand, watching with rapt attention as the butterfly circled erratically then landed on his palm.

He watched it for a few seconds, time slowing as it does for those who are soon to die. He felt none of the fear he normally had of such a creature. Instead his terror seemed to melt away and he was filled with a divine sense of wonder that such a beautiful thing should exist.

Marko gently curled his fingers shut, the butterfly passive to his touch. There was a bizarre comfort to the gossamer feel of this fragile and dying creature on his palm; he felt himself consoled, somehow—even—blessed.

The terror subsided.

Then, leaving only the slightest ripple, the tiniest eddy in the surface of the sea, Marko and the butterfly sank beneath the waves.

Going off the rails . . .

SPEED FREAKS

1

CYPRESS FOREST, HIDA MOUNTAIN RANGE, JAPAN
08:57 LOCAL TIME

The butterfly was an Alpine Grayling, a two-day-old creature living in a clearing in a pretty, protected valley of the Hida Mountain range in Japan.

This particular butterfly was a male, one of a late brood, hatching in the final moments of autumn warmth, and programmed by nature to feed, locate a female and mate—all in a ten day lifespan before the first chill nights of the coming winter would end the struggle for life.

Male butterflies are frequently territorial, they chase competitors away with a rising 'dance' that to an uneducated observer can look like a mating ritual.

The butterfly was dancing now, sparring with a rival which soon gave up the challenge and flew away into the forest. The Alpine Grayling descended to ground level and flitted among the wild flowers, feeding on the nectar with its long proboscis as bees and beetles jostled for space.

Then it sensed a threat; danger was in the air.

2

The butterfly collector was Professor Daichi Yamada, an entomologist from the Institute of Insect Systemization and Ecology in Osaka.

He was midway through his annual field trip, based in a tent way off the beaten track.

Yamada had set out alone at seven that morning with his net and collecting boxes. He was a fit man for a sixty year old: tramping around these rugged mountains was a routine working day for this white haired academic even if he often got lost along the way.

Now he was deep in a forested zone of cypress trees, searching for specimens which were missing from his collection.

He reached a clearing filled with flowers. Suddenly he saw it. An Alpine Grayling, a healthy looking specimen of the species which had for several years been on his hit list. The brown-coloured butterfly was darting around nervously, seeming to sense a hint of danger.

Yamada crept forward on his hands and knees. Midges and biting flies were buzzing around his ears and neck but their irritating stings were the last thing on his mind at that moment.

He held out the collecting net, stretching to the limit as the butterfly came tantalizingly close.

3

At that exact moment, halfway round the world, in the sweltering heat of a Rio night, a thirteen-year-old boy was struggling to get a huge load of rubbish onto his back. It was 10.15p.m. local time, an hour when more fortunate children would be safely tucked up in bed.

The kid was slight of frame, malnourished, in fact, with the watchful, prematurely adult eyes of a boy who suspects his life is worthless and who has seen too much cruelty at too young an age. His real name was Remo, but the people of the *favela* called him the 'pig-boy'.

The reason for the nickname was simple, Remo was one of the pigswill porters for the township, spending his time searching for rotting vegetables and other organic waste behind supermarkets and market stalls, then selling it for a pittance by the containerful to people who kept pigs in their gardens and yards.

The work was intensely physical and on occasions it was also downright dangerous; shopkeepers in the smarter parts of town didn't want the tone of their establishments lowered by kids like the 'pig-boy' rooting in their bins.

Sometimes they would set their guard dogs on him, just for fun. Remo had the scars on his calves to prove it.

4

The professor lunged forward, swiping the collecting net in a wild arc.

Missed. The Alpine Grayling dodged the mesh with a sudden swerve to the right.

He watched intently as the butterfly roamed from flower to flower. He moved the net forward once more. Then the creature seemed to realize it was being hunted, changing tactics as it suddenly rose several metres into the air.

The professor mopped sweat away from his eyes. He could have let it go but that wasn't Yamada's style. He was a doggedly determined man, and that species was one he had been searching for for several years.

The butterfly led the academic far from the clearing, into a zone of chest-high poplar bushes.

Yamada pushed his way into the dense thicket.

The butterfly descended. Nearly within reach. The professor jumped up, the mesh of his collecting net making a swishing noise in the air as he came within an ace of catching it.

Then he almost jumped out of his skin.

A black bear was sleeping right there in the thicket.

And the professor had just blundered into it.

He froze. But it was already too late.

The bear was awake. And it was mad as hell.

Suddenly it charged.

5

Back in Rio, a souped-up Hummer jeep was racing through the streets of the *favela*, thrash metal blasting on the stereo. The chunky vehicle was almost too big to squeeze through the alleys of the slum, the shanty buildings zooming past in a crazy flash of speed as the driver whooped and laughed with drunken pleasure.

A fifteen-year-old driver with no licence and a belly full of rum.

The vehicle was a real piece of work, a blinged-up bullet-proof monster which had cost more than two hundred thousand dollars. It was sprayed in gold, quartz pimp-lights studded into the alloys, smoked-glass windows protecting the occupants from curious eyes.

The owner of this travelling fortress was a man as dangerous as he was rich. Leonardo was one of Rio's more notorious drug barons, a cunning backstreet dealer who had got lucky and pulled off some huge deals. Now, thanks to a series of violent coups against his rivals he was king of the *favela*, a much-feared gangster with a small army of enforcers and dealers working for him.

The driver—Leonardo's son, Casio—was following enthusiastically in his father's dubious footsteps. He even mimicked Leonardo's look, with an intricate buzz cut hairstyle and razor striped brows.

'Don't be such a wimp!' Leonardo goaded his son. 'I don't want to see that speedo fall below sixty.'

Leonardo twisted the cap off a bottle of whisky and swigged hard on the liquor as Casio pushed the Hummer even harder down the dirty alleys. 'You're doing good,' Leonardo said, 'I'm proud of you, son.'

6

CYPRESS FOREST, HIDA MOUNTAIN RANGE, JAPAN

Yamada crashed through the thicket, the galloping bear rapidly gaining on him. It was phenomenally fast for such a huge creature.

Control the panic. Don't lose control.

Even as he ran, the professor was thinking what to do. Should he lie on the floor and play dead? Try to climb a tree? Keep running in the hope he could outpace the bear?

Maybe he should try and throw his rucksack?

Perhaps the bear would be distracted by it? Attack the rucksack instead of him?

But there was no time to shrug off the straps. If he slowed even fractionally the bear would catch him up. The professor risked a glance back. The bear was just a few metres behind him and it certainly didn't look as if it was going to give up the chase.

This was no bluff charge. The bad-tempered creature meant to teach this blundering human a lesson he would not forget.

The professor saw a cypress tree ahead. It had a low hanging branch which he might just reach if he jumped. He leaped for the branch, curling both hands around it...

7

At that instant in Tokyo, two hundred miles to the east, a fourteen-year-old girl called Saki arrived at the central railway station and boarded a Bullet Train for Nagano.

Saki was getting some curious looks from her fellow passengers:

It's not every day you see a pet rat on a train.

The rat was a two-year-old creature, sitting now on Saki's lap in its little cage. Its name was 'Brad'. Japanese girls are crazy about Mr Pitt.

Brad the Rat was of the type known as an Agouti Blue, its coat a dense black colour but spiked with attractive blue specks of hair. It was a healthy creature with gleaming dark eyes and a thickly scaled tail.

Saki liked to travel with her rat. Her parents had split up a year before, forcing her to shuttle backwards and forwards between her mother in Tokyo and her father in Nagano. She was bored to the back teeth with the Bullet Train and the creature was a welcome distraction even if it tended to freak other people out.

Saki was feeling thirsty. She needed a soda.

She picked up the little cage by its carrying handle and set off down the corridor towards the catering car.

As she did so she heard the doors shut with a gentle hiss.

The Bullet Train pulled out of the station and began to pick up speed.

8

Professor Yamada made it to the main trunk and scrambled awkwardly up to the highest point of the tree. He was quivering with nerves as he watched the angry bear pace backwards and forwards on the grass beneath him.

Would it try and climb the tree?

If it did he had no idea what he would do.

He forced himself to get his brain in check. A call. He had to get some help. Fast. He needed someone to come and shoot that bear before it killed him.

Yamada racked his brains. He knew he should call the police but how could he ask them for help when *he* didn't even know his exact location?

He would look a complete fool.

He did have a couple of clues. He could see the glittering water of a lake several kilometres away in the bottom of a valley. And next to it was a railway line. Yes! Yamada realized with a rush of satisfaction—it must be the main Tokyo to Nagano track.

It was a start. But would that information be enough to bring a rescue team to his aid?

The professor had no idea.

Then he remembered a colleague; a man who had studied Japanese bears for years. He might give some advice on how to handle the situation, advice that could save the professor's life.

Yamada selected his contacts folder to make the call.

9

The Hummer blitzed a trail through the slum, the two-tone horn blaring, sending roosting chickens squawking into the night. A couple of late-night revellers dived for a ditch as the vehicle roared past. Leonardo zapped down the window and fired his pistol into the sky, the ripe stench of rotting rubbish filling his nostrils as he breathed in the night air.

'Wake up, losers!' Leonardo screamed. 'There's no time to sleep!'

Casio slammed the Hummer into top gear, a big grin splitting his young face. It was shaping up into a great night.

Just an hour or so earlier, Casio and his thuggish mates had been downtown, targeting a family of rich American tourists eating at one of Rio's late-night food malls. There were two young boys with the family, both laden with attractive gadgets and innocent as new-born lambs.

Casio and his gang had waited until the two boys went to the rest room, cornered them there, slapped them around a bit and mugged them of their toys.

The thugs had split the spoils: Casio—the ringleader—coming out of it with the American kids' iPhone and a state of the art MP4 player.

The look of raw fear on the kids' faces had been a buzz. Sure, they were only eleven or twelve years old, but it still made Casio feel like a real gangster.

He loved that rush. There was nothing like it.

10

The recipient of the professor's call was Dr Roger Stansfield, and at that moment he was sitting with a coffee in seat 11b in car number two of the Nagano-bound Bullet Train.

Stansfield was one of Yamada's closest colleagues, a native of Dublin in Ireland who had married a Japanese girl many years ago, learned the language, and settled into academic life as a biologist in Nagano.

Stansfield gave a little sigh as he saw who was calling him. Yamada was a bit of a joke in the staff room but Stansfield had a soft spot for the old academic even if he was scatterbrained to the point of distraction.

'Roger.' Yamada sounded out of breath and his voice was indistinct. 'I'm... (pause) a tree... (pause) with a bear... (pause)... helicopter.'

The line was a bad one, continually cutting out. 'What? I can't hear you. Did you say something about a... *bear*?'

Then the call went dead.

Stansfield tutted to himself as he thought this through. The call had been mystifying to say the least. Did Yamada say 'bear'... and 'helicopter'?

The academic decided he would call Yamada back, but he didn't want to make the call from his seat where the conversation would excite interest from his fellow travellers.

He rose abruptly from his seat but he forgot about the coffee sitting on the small table in front of him.

The drink went flying into the aisle.

11

Remo the 'pig-boy' turned down a sewage-filled alley and found the bins of a fast-food restaurant. Years working in the dark had given him phenomenal night vision. He was using the faint glimmer of starlight to help him sift through the waste.

There was plenty of good food there for pigs: half-eaten pizza crusts, rock-hard rinds of mouldy cheese, withered old potatoes which were soggy to the touch.

Remo got to work. Filling up his sack.

As he worked he thought about his mother, lying sick in a tumbledown hut on the other side of town. Her working days as a factory cleaner were over; her lungs riddled with disease. Remo's father Carlito was no longer around; he'd gone to sea on a cargo ship two years earlier and they'd never heard a word since.

There was no safety net for the inhabitants of the *favela*. No sickness benefit. No government support. Neighbours could be kind, but how often can you ask for help from people who have themselves got nothing?

That was why Remo had started up the waste collecting. Without the few coins he brought home every Sunday his mother would starve to death. That was the hard reality of life in the *favela*.

Remo longed to leave the stinking little tin shack where he lived. Sometimes he fantasized about taking his mother back to the sugar cane plantation where she had

spent her childhood. The stories she told about that place . . .
it seemed like a sweet heaven, clean sheets, hot food . . .

A scabby dog growled at him from the shadows.

Dream on, he thought. *Get real.* This is how it's always
going to be.

12

SHINKANSEN BULLET TRAIN,
EN-ROUTE NAGANO, JAPAN

Saki was walking down the aisle of car number two, heading
for the catering car, when the anxious looking man with the
mobile suddenly shot up from his seat.

His Styrofoam cup of coffee tipped, then fell into the
aisle . . . and right over the carrying cage containing Saki's
pet rat.

The rat jumped back in shock as the scalding liquid hit its back.

Saki unclipped the catch and opened the little door to the
cage. She reached in for the rat and took it firmly in her
hand. The little rodent was scared half to death, hissing
with fear as the pain of the scalding coffee overwhelmed it.
Saki took off her scarf and dabbed at the rat's fur to try to
remove the liquid.

'OK, my little one.' She tried to soothe the rat with a few
calming words.

Then it happened.

Brad the Rat bit Saki on the thumb. He'd never done that before.

'Ow!' Saki pulled her hand back fast in a reflex reaction.

*The rat dropped to the floor and ran down the central aisle of
the wagon.*

About the author

Matt Dickinson is a writer and film maker with an enduring (and sometimes dangerous) passion for wild places and even wilder people. He was trained at the BBC and has subsequently filmed many award-winning documentaries for National Geographic television, Discovery Channel and Channel 4.

As a director/cameraman he has worked with some of the world's top climbers and adventurers, joining them on their expeditions to the Himalayas and beyond. Along the way he has survived some life-threatening dramas; an avalanche in Antarctica, a killer storm on Everest and a night-time 'grizzly bear' attack in the Yukon which wasn't quite what it seemed (actually they were beavers!).

Matt's proudest moment was filming on the summit of Mount Everest having successfully scaled the treacherous north face of the world's highest peak.

www.mortalchaos.com